HELLO
NOW

Also by Jenny Valentine

FIRE COLOR ONE

Jenny Valentine

PHILOMEL

Philomel Books
An imprint of Penguin Random House LLC, New York

First published in the United States of America by Philomel,
an imprint of Penguin Random House LLC, 2020.
First published in Great Britain by HarperCollins in 2020.

Philomel Books is a registered trademark of Penguin Random House LLC.

Visit us online at penguinrandomhouse.com

LIBRARY OF CONGRESS CATALOGING-IN-PUBLICATION DATA
Names: Valentine, Jenny, author.
Title: Hello now / Jenny Valentine.
Description: New York : Philomel Books, 2020. | Audience: Ages 12 up. |
Audience: Grades 7–9. | Summary: "The story of an out-of-time romance
between Jude and Novo, two teens looking for a way to connect to the
world"—Provided by publisher.
Identifiers: LCCN 2019030844 (print) | LCCN 2019030845 (ebook) |
ISBN 9780399546952 (hardcover) | ISBN 9780399546969 (epub)
Subjects: CYAC: Time travel—Fiction. | Love—Fiction. | Gays—Fiction. |
Moving, Household—Fiction.
Classification: LCC PZ7.V25213 Hel 2020 (print) | LCC PZ7.V25213 (ebook)
| DDC [Fic]—dc23
LC record available at https://lccn.loc.gov/2019030844
LC ebook record available at https://lccn.loc.gov/2019030845

Printed in the United States of America
ISBN 9780399546952
1 3 5 7 9 10 8 6 4 2

Edited by Liza Kaplan.
Design by Victoria Lee.
Text set in ITC Caslon 224 Std.

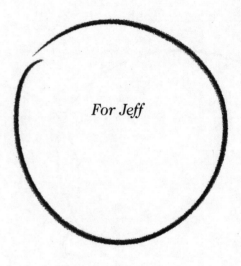

For Jeff

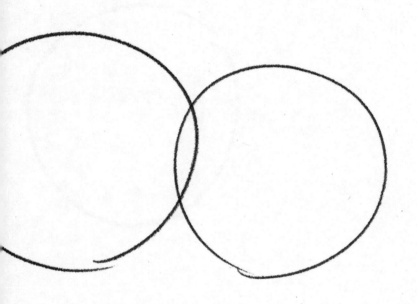

HELLO
NOW

Novo

When it happens, I don't feel it. I never feel it. I just sleep. And they wash away, the things I've held on to, all of them. I let them go, leave them unchanged, and they are clean and new and nothing and then I am back. Never the same place— sometimes the cut and pulse of human traffic, sometimes a vast empty space. Anywhere and Always. The hot bite of dust, a blanket of snow. Soft opening of a morning or deep, sharp night. Sometimes before Now, and during, and also after, just the land holding bodies and the birds rising up over the sea. Square one, in all its different disguises. Always moving. Always alone.

I never forget what I am looking for, over and over, some-where in that black-hole sleep. The one that keeps me. The one

I can keep. My hook. A face at a window, the air in a bubble, a bird in a cage. Consequence. Purpose. Belonging.

A street. Here. Now.

Will it be this time? Will it be never? I get out of the car, know my name and my age, my own hands, all my histories, same as ever. Quiet facts come to me like old finger drawings on glass, only traces. These trees. This house. This beginning. I stand at the side of the road, taking it all in, hoping and hoping. And I wonder, not for the first time, if it has some kind of start, this life, and who's controlling it, and if it is ever, ever going to stop.

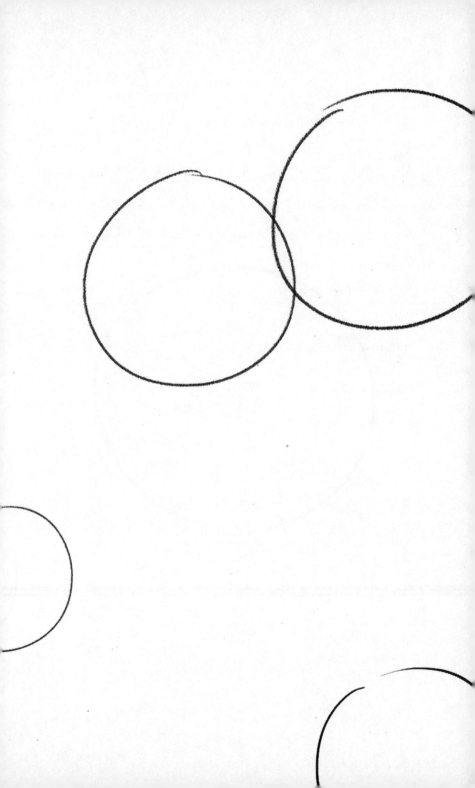

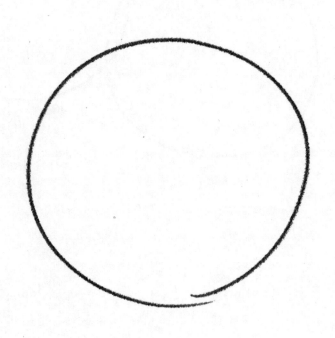

ONE

Jude

I've never been into love stories. Too much sugar, too much gloop, same reasons I don't like cotton candy or fondue. Only so many sunsets and hand-holds and ever-afters I can stomach, honestly. Seven words for it in Greek. Twenty-seven in Tamil. All those subtleties and we just have this one four-letter word and expect everyone to make a religion out of it.

I've never been into magic either, not the made-up, miracle kind. Not when there's the miracle of actually existing to deal with, the magic of infinitely small particles, the exact same particles, coming together to make a human being or a seashell or the earth's atmosphere or a cup of tea or just a log. There's magic in putting one foot in front of the other, isn't there?

There's magic in a foot, come to think of it. It's everywhere. Even to be here is so much.

That's what I knew about love before, when it was still just a spectator sport for me. Here's what I learned by osmosis. That people spend their time wishing so hard to be with someone else, they forget how to be a proper version of themselves. That we are all too ready to give up our independence, ache to hand it over gladly like it's nothing, and make someone else responsible for our happiness, someone way less invested, way less qualified than us.

That kind of love is a selfish thing, transactional, an exalted kind of laziness, and that's why nobody says "I love you" without wanting it said back.

But love is not a transaction. Four-letter love is a big black hole and that's why you fall into it. The finest bubble, the best dream, where you don't want to wake up, not for a second, not ever, because you know you have to, you know you will, and that then, nothing else will come close. It makes all the everyday miracles duller and more ordinary, just from having been there, from having gone. That kind of love and magic feel the same. I know that now, for a fact. I'm an expert on the things I used to say didn't exist.

Other loves aren't a difficult ask for me. I love my mother. That goes without saying, even when I don't like her. I love London, and my old house and all the days of my childhood, all my friends. I love the sea, and walking on its edges, and the taste of salt and vinegar on a hot french fry. I love dancing in dark rooms and getting lost in a long book, and you've got to love laughing, everybody loves a decent joke. I love strangers and the internet and I love snow and sand and new places. I love obvious signs of loneliness, for some reason, and old people and young people and most dogs and the things we say to each other and singing and all types of fire and the underdog and a lot of movies, even bad ones, and marmalade on dry brown toast and clean sheets and ginger tea and I am really only just getting started.

Love is everywhere too.

I could fill this whole page with the things I love. I could carry on thinking of new ones without stopping, twenty-four hours a day, until I die. But all of them, standing together, armed to the teeth and in organized ranks with me leading the charge, still couldn't have prepared me for Novo. Of having him. Of having him with me, alone, the great weight of his arm. And then not.

When I think about that, I feel the impact in my chest, the air pushed from my lungs, the clean sharp break of all the bones in my body. It hurts. It's a violent equation, love plus loss. I don't want that to be true. But I don't know how else I'm supposed to put it.

Look how hard it hit me. I'm bleeding love story all over the place.

TWO

In the beginning, before I knew that I didn't know much about anything, my mum and I moved into a house with a stranger in it. It was a big house in the small town she grew up in (and then left, by the way, swearing never to return) on a street where fat-knuckled trees pulled at the pavements with their roots, and the average age was well over fifty, and nobody said very much.

The stranger wasn't hiding in the attic or lurking under the floorboards. He wasn't a blind purchase. His name was Henry Lake, and he came with the sale, refusing to budge. A sitting tenant, Mum said. A fly in the freeholder's ointment. A stick in the capitalist mud. "Something we can both get behind," she said, which I told her was optimistic, and at the time, frankly, pushing it.

She remembered the street from her childhood, sort of, and that the houses were beautiful. And massive. And had yards that sloped right down to the sea. This meant less than nothing to me—five hours' drive from my current definition of home—and I told her that too. But because of this stranger still living in it, this house on the sole of the boot of the country was a whole lot cheaper than anything else she'd managed to find. Thanks to Henry Lake being there, it was the one she could afford, so it was happening, we were going, end of discussion, and that was that. It's thanks to him and because of him that so much other stuff happened too, and is still happening, but I'm getting ahead of myself, and when I started writing this down, that's one of the things I swore I wouldn't do. This particular love story is bewildering enough as it is without me helping.

We didn't have a separate front door or anything. Henry Lake's rooms were on the middle floor, and we were just meant to move in and live around him like the white surrounds the yolk of an egg. I said that was flat-out ridiculous, and when Mum told me to get used to it, every cell in my body screamed *never*.

"Seriously?" I said. "No locks on the doors? What are you thinking? What if he's unhinged? For all we know he could be a killer," and while I was saying it, something dark scuttled down an alley in my stomach, this idea that I might be right, that this was my fate, set already, bound to happen. Game over. Job done.

"Plus it's miles away," I said again, into the void Mum left by not responding. "No joke, Mum. You've lost your actual mind."

"No, Jude," she said, folding into her chair like a dropped flag. "I've lost everything else."

Everything else translated loosely as Mark, her boyfriend for just under a year, her latest Holy Grail, her answer to just about every question under the sun. Mark wasn't all that, but he was all right. He was pretty nice to her and he didn't act like I was the unwanted guest or the icing on the cake, unlike some previous boyfriends I could mention. He worked in insurance and you'd think from the way she batted her eyelashes at him when he droned on about assets and premiums that a man in insurance was all she'd ever wanted, the sum total of her heart's desires. My mum is a very good actor. She couldn't give a shit about insurance. What she wants is not to be alone.

Anyway, Mark had taken his assets and premiums elsewhere, and because he was also our landlord, that included the roof over our heads. Mum was still in phase one, acting like it was the end of the world, which it blatantly wasn't. She was doing that thing she does where she just takes for granted that it's me and her against the world, without even asking if I was on her side for this one. She said, "Can you believe this is even happening to us?" and when I pointed out it was actually her decision to drop everything and drag me to a sad-sounding, pensioner-dense, end-of-the-road, far-as-the-eye-could-see whites-only seaside town from her distant past, she welled up and went all defense-less wounded puppy on me, because it works every time and she knows it. Takes the sting right out of my fight.

"A new start," she called it, without asking me if I even wanted one, because it was obvious I didn't, and I said, "Haven't we had our share of those?" One for every Mark that turned out not to be God's gift after all. Such an over-investor. She might as well have invented the concept of eggs in one basket. Eight full new starts, and three or four half-hearted versions, where I didn't have to move schools at least, just took way longer to get there and was always late for everything, always left behind. It was always like that, since my dad, I guess, who was the first but who came and went just like the others. A link in a chain, and a stranger now. If I saw him in the street I wouldn't know him. Sad but true. I've made my peace with that.

This time, phase-one Mum was really shaking things up. Maybe I should have been more positive. She was doing it by herself, after all. Declaring independence. But at the time, she knew how I felt about it. I reminded her it had taken work to make even the few friends I had. I said we both knew there was no way I'd be able to keep them, not at that distance. I wanted that to count for something. I was looking for mercy, but that well was dry.

"You'll get new friends," she said, like I could just pick some out in a gift shop, like that was how easy it was, and it stunned me, the ignorance, the carelessness of that.

"Ouch," I said. "Blunt."

"What?" she said. "You're good at it."

"Yeah? Because I've had to be."

"Well, life teaches us the skills we need," she said, trying to make a virtue out of throwing me in at the social deep end every time a new Prince Charming withered on the vine.

When I was eight and we were moving for the third time in a year (a real bad patch—Jim, I think, then Danny, then Joe), I tried to stop the move from happening by tying everything in my room down with string. I got a ball of it and I cat's-cradled the hell out of my bed and my radiator and my toy cupboard and my bookshelf and then I waited like Charlotte in the middle of her web to see what I'd spelled. Mum used to tell that story to people like it was funny. I've heard it a hundred times over the years, and I've smiled and nodded and put up with being laughed at. She even laughed at me when it happened. She opened the door and she opened her mouth and threw her head back and I could see the undersides of her teeth, the biting edges, and I remember thinking, *How could she?* because it was the opposite of funny, to me. I was dead scared of losing something. I didn't want things to change. Not again. But they did, and they do, and I guess I started learning way back then that you can't stop your world from turning, however tight you tie it down, however hard you try.

So. Here we were again. Move number thirteen. Mum was on her own, not counting me. She was acting out and we were packing up and I was all set to repeat, all set to be brand-new in another place. I could feel it coming—the unknown, the sudden onset of lonely. First-world problems, sure, but still. Problems all the same.

THREE

The estate agents and lawyers weren't above making the prospect of this Henry Lake's death a kind of sweetener on the deal. Our sitting tenant was old, apparently, and not in great shape, and I heard one of them tell Mum on the phone that she wouldn't have too long to wait to get the whole house to herself. A euphemism if ever I heard one. "Health problems," he said, the same way he probably said "detached garage" and "en suite bathroom." I listened and I sat on my hands and tried to laugh, which is the only way to deal with outrage sometimes, the only safe way to breathe out and be gentle and just watch it pass.

When she hung up I said, "Isn't it a hundred different kinds of not right that a real-life, living person would make a place worth less money instead of more? Don't you think?" but Mum was still in high-drama, post-breakup crisis mode. She said, "I've got other things to think about, Jude, more immediate and pressing things, like finding a real place to live." And I suppose I've got more immediate and pressing things to say now, and that's part of the trouble, and why the value of a human life ends up having to wait for later.

Last Supper time in the flat, she pushed spaghetti hoops around on her plate instead of eating them, one of those new role-reversal moments that made me want to tell her to sit up properly and stop playing with her food.

"Don't worry," she said without commitment, kind of absent behind the eyes, like she had been for a while. "Everything's going to be fine. Mr. Lake is a nice man on a nice street."

"Yeah. So was Ted Bundy," I said, and for a second I thought she might crack a smile, but she didn't, just scowled, like I was trying to trick her into it.

She stood up to scrape the rest of her spaghetti hoops into the trash, the back of her head more expressive of her feelings than you'd think possible. Just a nudge and the whole lot slid off the plate in one slimy clump, a colony of something, half-reluctant, half-alive, which put me right off finishing mine. I watched her grip on the fork, waited for her knuckles to go from bone-light back to skin, and then I asked her again why a house was worth less money with another human being inside it, how that could ever be allowed to happen. On a good day, that might have been the start of a proper conversation about plutocracies and trickle-down economics and the politics of homeownership and the poverty gap, and I would have learned something. But we weren't back to good days yet. No such luck.

"Oh, you know," she said without turning round. "It's the way of the world. People don't like to share," like that nailed it, like it was all that needed to be said.

"Is that it?" I said, and she said, "Pick your side, Jude. Is he a human being or an unhinged killer?"

"Or both," I said, and she glared at me and the angry pulse in her jaw ticked.

"This is the last time, Mum. I'm not doing this with you again, I swear."

"Fine with me," she said on her way out of the room, but neither of us meant it, not really, and that was another one of our new-style low-quality splinter-family mealtimes over and done with.

FOUR

On the drive down, I'd had less than two hours of sleep, and no breakfast. The air-conditioning in the car had been broken since forever and the stereo was playing up. Mum said, "If it rains, we're screwed," because the windshield wipers were worn out and basically useless. She wasn't even sure if the car was going to start, or keep it together long enough to get us there, so on top of not wanting to go, there was the stress of not knowing if we'd actually arrive.

"Yay," I said. "Road trip."

I can't read in a moving car because it makes me want to throw up. In fact, it's just about the only place on the planet where a good book does nothing for me, my own special version of hell. I'd dropped my phone the week before, third time in as many months, and it was properly smashed, no real hope of repair, tiny hidden cogs and chips exposed like so much guts, close to useless in terms of in-car entertainment. I'd tried wrapping it up with tape to hold all its innards together, and the camera still worked, on and off, but it was like looking at everything through a shattered glass eye and half the time it just froze and stared me out like it was annoyed with me, which it probably was. Mum said she wasn't paying for another one because I was (quote) pathologically incapable of looking after it, and she was twenty-four hours a day losing her shit about money anyway, so, job done.

Out past the M25, I told her about my (about to be ex) friend Roma's grandad telling us out of the blue that he'd been an extra in the original *Star Wars*. And about this film I'd seen online about how the advertising industry got inside everyone's heads in the 1950s thanks to some pioneering PR guy who was related to Freud. And about a book I'd started reading about the history of the atmosphere. All perfect openers, in my opinion, and there was a time they'd have worked like a charm, but this wasn't one of them. Mum wasn't biting, so I got desperate and asked her who her favorite Simpson was. That's when she breathed out through her mouth like a cross horse and told me to be quiet for *just one minute* if that was at all possible, so she could *think*.

Rude.

Most of the known world says that people my age are hard to communicate with, but really? They should try getting through to my mother when she's driving. The silence that descended was familiar, well-worn, the wonder-what-(insert name here)-is-doing-now-and-who-with silence. I looked the other way out of the window after that, kept my mouth shut out of principle, missing home—the phone shops and the flower stall, the dry cleaners and the tube station and the fried chicken place whose window was always broken, never fixed, not for long anyway. The view from the road felt spare and oddly empty. There wasn't much else to look at on the way down but fields and other cars and clouds and sky.

It didn't rain, and the car got us there in one piece, and even though I wasn't grateful, I could see straight off that the street was way tidier than we were used to, another level—quiet and wide and tree-lined, high up in the town with a view of the sea, pure blue that day, same as the sky. No traffic jams. No autopsied mopeds or abandoned fridges, no weatherproof all-season dog shit or stained mattresses or boarded-up windows. A sharp salt smell and this strong bright light and palm trees. Palm trees. The wind leaned hard against the car like it didn't want us to get out, knew right away that we didn't belong. *Turn back*, it said, *big mistake, don't even think about stopping*, and I still wonder sometimes what life would be like if Mum had heard it, if she'd turned the car around and just obeyed. I let out a low whistle and watched her force the dark back down in her eyes. I know she felt it suddenly, the impact of her decision, right then, middle-aged and anti-climaxed, with me in tow. Not what you'd call triumphant. Not exactly a lap of honor. If I'd known what to say to her then, what would have helped, I like to think I might have said it. But then again, maybe not. We should all be given a manual at birth for that sort of thing.

I started fishing around under my seat for the steering wheel lock, and she said, "I wouldn't bother, Jude. No one's going to pick on our heap-of-crap car in this ocean of high-quality metal," and she had a point. The low-budget new neighbors had definitely arrived.

We got out. The wind whipped my hair into my mouth and back out again, turned Mum's jacket into an airbag. The house with Henry Lake in it stood out as much as we did, a stain on the neat white terrace like a rotten tooth. All manner of crap was crammed in the trashcans and stuffed in the uncut hedges. The roof was pockmarked with moss and weeds and bird shit. Some clever kind of tree had taken root up there, getting a head start on all the others, and I had some respect for that. Henry Lake's elongated shadow scuttled across an upstairs window. A gull on the chimney pot opened its throat and cried, launching itself into the air above our heads. I heard the sail-crack of its wings, saw its rain-cloud underside as it circled, head tilted, gimlet-eyed, watching. I hate being the center of attention. I could feel the blood needling in my fingers, the jittering bones in my ears. I liked our old life. I liked our last apartment. I knew how to get there from my friends' houses, from all the places we went out. I knew where every single thing was kept. Me and Mum and Mark were happy there, sort of, until we weren't. It had been an okay place to call home. And it didn't have an old stranger curled up in the middle of it, like a maggot in a peach.

"I hate this," I told her.

"Me too," she said, and she tried to put her arm round me, mark the occasion like we were in it together, but I dodged out of range and left her hanging, because in that moment I felt like my eight-year-old self with that ball of string, and that feeling made me angry.

If we were back there, arriving at Henry's again, if it was happening now, I would do so much better than that. I would remember that sometimes, the thing you've dreaded the most can be the actual making of you, the thing you would never end up trading for all the money or fame or love or good fortune in the world. I would take my old self to one side and tell them straight out that one of the best things about the unknown is that it's 100 percent guaranteed to surprise you. Every time.

FIVE

Mum rang the bell and knocked on the front door, even though we had our own key. She said it was the right thing to do, but when Henry Lake didn't answer, she gave up on the right thing pretty quickly and we let ourselves in. Her favorite mug has a Groucho Marx quote on it: *These are my principles, and if you don't like them . . . well, I have others.* I shoplifted it for her one Christmas (using the principle of common ownership) and she has no idea, but that's a whole different can of worms. This can of worms was Henry Lake, who must have felt rather than heard the key in the lock and the mortise rolling open and us standing there underneath him in the empty hall, waiting for the next great big chapter in our lives to begin.

Inside, the house was quiet and full of echoes, kind of dank, like a cave. High ceilings and low lighting. Room after room, full of nothing. Dark, bad-weather-gray walls, old floorboards the color of pricey honey. The hallway alone was bigger than the whole downstairs of our old flat. In a room at the back, a slice of window filled with nothing but the petrol-blue sea, churning and hypnotic, oddly silent behind the glass. Henry Lake came out of his room and stood over us at the top of the staircase, a man steeling himself to make any kind of entrance. If Mum was hoping for shining armor, she was disappointed. He was old as hell and oddball perfect. Stooped over, kind of tall, apologetic almost, bone thin. His jeans hung from his hips like they were empty on a peg, like half of him had already given up and started disappearing. Sunglasses, even in that gloom, and a faded black baseball cap pulled down low as it would go over the bridge of his nose. Out of its shadow, the rest of his face was just gray beard. There was a rhythm to the way he took the stairs, a deliberate thump that bounced off the walls and made the light fixtures tremble. Over that, I could hear the music still playing in his ears, distant and tinny, a dropped box of pins on repeat, headphones the size of ear defenders over the top of his cap. He didn't turn it down or take any of it off, just stood there in full disguise, full armor, insulated against our normal, whatever that was. There was no way of telling who he was under there. It occurred to me for a second that he might be wildly famous, because only a proper celebrity would meet someone for the first time and try to get away with a look as batshit as that.

"You're here," he said, and Mum said, "Yes."

"Good," he said. "Welcome. I've been waiting."

Surrounded by all that sober wood, the dust thick and dancing in pockets of sunlight, Mum introduced herself, and I scowled and waved like some dumb teenager from central casting, and Henry Lake smiled. At least I think he did. Something moved under that beard anyway. I could hear him chewing, the regular, elastic squelch of his gum, the pulse in his forehead going like a metronome. He made a break-ice comment about the weather, and it was obvious he'd rehearsed it, for something to say, and that he had nothing else to follow it with, nothing prepared. It's a terrible thing when some people make small talk—like seeing a wild animal in a sweater. Mum said something back, something optimistic about the quality of the light, and when that died a death, we just stood there in silence and it was pure tumbleweed—pure, undiluted awkward. I felt sick. My hangover was a stealth one. The kind that wakes you up fine, lulls you into a false sense of security, and then waits till you're fully immersed in your day before it decides to pin you down and kick you in the teeth. I wanted to go to my room and get into bed, but neither of those things existed anymore, not in the same way, and that just made me want them even more.

Look at us in that Now. Mum and Henry Lake radiating strangeness and dashed hopes, trying to dredge up something to say to each other, and me with the sudden homesick cold sweats, malfunction-malfunction.

A bell rang upstairs somewhere, and Henry said, "Must go," and I was like, *Where?* as he bowed to both of us, shallow and quick, like a butler, and went back up the stairs. I heard his door open and shut and Mum closed her eyes and breathed out.

"Well, that went well," she said, and I said, "Yeah. I don't know what I've been worrying about all this time," and I went outside and sat on the doorstep, hoping someone from my old life would drive by and save me.

Across the road, an ambulance arrived, sirens off, no great hurry, and a nurse came out of the house opposite and stood on the doorstep in the swaying shade of a rose and ushered the paramedics in.

"Mrs. Midler," Henry said from his place at the window above me, leaning, elbows on the sill. "She's the last of them."

I looked up. "Last of who?" I said.

The nurse shut the front door and Henry said, "The old guard. All new here now. All change," and he was already moving back in, already pulling on the sash window with his stick-thin arms, the skin on them rippled and half-see-through like a forgotten balloon.

Not long after that, the moving van rumbled up to meet our car nose to nose. "Mum," I said. "The Freak Brothers are here," and the men who'd stripped our apartment like locusts the day before dropped onto the tarmac in their matching red T-shirts and caps, trailing fat clouds of weed. They opened the back and it made this gunshot noise in the quiet street that ricocheted off the housefronts and upset the seagulls.

"Welcome to our Family Museum," I told them as they wheeled and cawed in the blue, watching the men unload. "Roll up, roll up for a show of our worldly goods."

Exhibits included one scrubbed table and four stained chairs. An old pavement-colored meat cupboard and the top, non-business half of an old pinball machine. Our dented fridge, ink-black with mold in certain places and still stuck somehow with a sea of alphabet magnets that pooled together to spell jUDe!*?! and BY m0Re M1Lk FfS and then broke apart again into chaos.

Two cheap flattened beds and Mum's high-backed armchair, a plan chest, an invasion of trash bags (clothes, basically), boxes of books, and some stuff in bubble wrap—that one mirror, that one canvas, that one I couldn't even remember anymore. The men in red walked everything up the path, tendons straining, teeth gritted, and in through the stale, narrow mouth of our new front door. It wasn't nearly enough to make a dent on a house that size. The things we owned sat marooned in each sea of room, washed up and adrift, just like wreckage. Just like us.

Out on the street, the movers climbed back into the truck and slammed the doors, and after that the paramedics wheeled Mrs. Midler out of the house opposite on a gurney with the blanket pulled up over her head. Everything was dead quiet, apart from the blunt sound of her rattling down the front path and off the curb. It took them three tries to get the ambulance doors shut, and the noise spun the gulls off the roofs, kick-started a dog-barking relay two streets away, woke up a couple of babies in their strollers somewhere, and life began again, just like that.

Henry Lake dropped something upstairs and it broke and he swore, and the scrape and rustle of him clearing it up above me was like a haunting. Less sitting tenant somehow, more house-bound ghost. I wondered how long he had lived there, and what he'd meant, exactly, by the old guard, and how he felt about us just moving right in, and how many other people he'd watched come and go from his place in the middle of that house. The way of things, I know, the ebb and flow, but still, relentless.

SIX

Later, my arms were full and I was trying to navigate the landing when I went backward through the wrong door into Henry's private territory. Two airless rooms divided by frosted glass doors, the shapes of unmade bed and heaped-up chair on one side, and when I turned, a skeletal chandelier listing from the ceiling, a table that looked like someone had emptied a filing cabinet and about a month's worth of dishes onto it. A portrait of a dark-haired woman, just her naked back and her long neck, her face about to turn to show her profile, but just out of reach, and that forever-not-quite caught my attention. At the other end, a half-assed kind of kitchen, an antique fridge the color of old custard, and an angry, worn-out straw-yellow parakeet in a cage. Things that might have enjoyed some spread in the rest of the house were sardined into this one cramped, chaotic space. I had this sense of Henry and all his stuff gathered there, in the center, the way the pupil of your eye retracts in bright light. Three huge wardrobes stood side by side, giants waiting for a bus. A sofa suffocated under piles of old maps and notebooks, no space left on it to sit, a lidless pen bleeding ink into its grubby cushions. Above that was the biggest map of the world I've ever seen, stuck with hundreds of tiny pins. The paintwork was a lumpy, tobacco-stain kind of white, and the floorboards were covered with newspaper and boot prints and bird shit. Something on the stove top smelled like boiled chicken, rich and strong and kind of everywhere. I wondered how the caged bird felt about that. It stared at me, and so did Henry Lake. Two pairs of eyes. One quick-black bird-lacquer, the other, without sunglasses this time, mind-bendingly tired. I don't think I'd ever seen anyone look more exhausted. I didn't want to look at him for too long, in case it was catching.

"Sorry," I said. "Wrong door," and the parakeet twitched.

Henry Lake smiled and wiped his hands on a stained tea towel. He moved to sweep half the contents of the sofa straight onto the floor. "No, come in. Excuse the mess. It's been ages since I had a visitor."

Out of politeness more than anything, I put the stuff I'd been carrying down by the door, setting off an epic cloudburst of dust, and I sat on the edge of the sofa while the little bird shivered in its cage and Henry searched for something in the kitchen.

"Do you like olives?" he said, not exactly hanging on an answer. "I've got a jar somewhere."

"I'm all right," I said.

"Tea? Soup? I'm making soup."

"I don't need anything. I'm fine."

"Hungry work, I'd have thought," he said, "moving."

"I'm used to it."

"Lucky you," he said, and I rolled my eyes.

"If you say so."

"Are you furious?" he asked me, and I wasn't expecting that question, so I was honest. I didn't have time to hide my answer behind anything, to cover it up.

"Yeah," I said. "I am, sort of. I hate change."

In the silence that followed he went back to poking at the keyboard of a clunky old laptop. The ancient fridge hummed. The bird fussed. My asthma was starting up, that wet wheeze like chunks of my breath being passed through a sieve. I am allergic to dust. It makes my eyes burn and my nose run and my lungs block all the exits, and it is everywhere, I know, but that old house was the Mothership, the source of its Nile. I used my inhaler and concentrated on breathing, and I had another look around while Henry tapped away. The back wall was covered in clocks, different shapes and sizes, not one of them set to the same time. All that ticking sounded like rain dripping somewhere on a roof.

"Change," Henry Lake said, "is unavoidable. Essential. It's the engine of everything."

"I know," I said, because I hadn't meant it at an atomic level, I'd just meant the my-mum, emotional-rebound kind of change.

"Imagine life without it," he said. "A rock in a stream."

"Rocks change," I said. "The water changes them," and Henry smiled.

"You're a smart one, aren't you. I can see we are going to be friends."

"Friends are a bit of a sore topic for me," I said.

"It'll pass," said Henry. "Life will provide."

"You reckon?"

"I'm an unspeakably old man," he said.

"So?"

"So I've seen it enough times to know."

"I haven't," I said.

"But you will."

It was quiet then, and I looked at the woman's portrait again, the smooth skin of her back, her turning head. I looked at her for a long time.

"I do like that painting," I said, and he smiled.

"Lifetimes since I did that."

"*You* did it?"

"I used to love to paint," he said. "A very long time ago. And then a very long time ago, I gave it up."

Some tiny part of me believed the woman in the portrait might actually turn around. I remember thinking how silly that was, that I felt like that, even in that moment. "She's very lovely."

"Yes." Henry frowned and carried on typing. "She was."

He turned the laptop screen toward me, some kind of aerial view. Wild dust, scrubby trees, a shrunk river. A pack of dogs crossed the picture from bottom corner to top. Tall slanted shadows, left to right. "Look at this," he said. "Today, we're on the savanna."

"Today?"

"Yes. See?" He got up and pointed to the giant wall map. "Sub-Saharan Africa. About here." He put a pin in it.

"Have you been to all of those places?" I said. "With all of those pins?"

The estate agents had called Henry Lake a recluse. They hadn't mentioned anything about world travel.

"In a manner of speaking," he said.

"What manner?"

He didn't answer me. Not directly. He said, "Have you ever seen these dogs in the wild?"

"Me? Nope. Never been anywhere. Not like that. I don't even know what kind of dogs they are."

"Well," he said, flourishing his hands like a magician at the end of a trick. "There. Painted dogs. You've seen them now."

"Yes, but we're not *in the wild*, are we. We're not actually there."

Henry reached out a hand to touch the screen. "We work with what we have," he said. "There's more than one way to see the world these days."

"Okay," I said. "If you say so."

The look on his face was kind of pleading. He so wanted to be right. "Those dogs are moving across that ground right now. Right this minute. Look. Isn't that something? Isn't that good enough?"

He typed something into the filthy keyboard and the picture zoomed, close up, a dog moving low to the ground, ears turning like satellite dishes, mouth dripping chewed foam and a grin. I remember the stark, strong shadows and the dogs' tongues lolling, and I might have heard the ragged sounds of their breath. I can't have felt the blunt heat of the air, the greasy nap of their fur. Still, my memory fills in those blanks for me anyway, and those dogs seem hyperreal now to me.

"How does it work?" I said. "Do you just shut your eyes and stick a pin in the wall?"

"Something like that."

"Right."

"Modern technology. It's a tremendous help for someone like me."

"Someone like you?"

"I can't get out," Henry Lake said.

"What, ever?"

He shook his head. "It's more trouble than it's worth."

"Really?"

I wanted to know how he lived like that. Where did his food come from? What happened if he got sick? And I wanted to know *why* too, more than anything, but I'd only just met him, so I was nervous to ask. Mum started calling me from downstairs, fifth-gear annoyed with me already—something about a chest of drawers, something about my skateboard being a death trap, something else about me lifting a finger to help.

"You'd better go," he said, and I picked up my boxes from where I'd left them by the door, and our conversation was over.

Henry hunched down closer at his table, a world traveler under house arrest, with his elbow in a plate of dried sauce, his gnarled, papery hand scratching at the roots of his beard. One foot in the savanna, the other trapped in the yolk of an egg.

SEVEN

I helped Mum do a few things, and then I got away as soon as I could, on my own for the first time all day. Upstairs, my new room in the attic was a mixed bag, two parts brilliant, two parts the opposite of that. It was the place where all the flies came to die. I watched them flitting and buzzing at the windows like crowds at the turnstiles, exiting their weightless corpses across the sills and along the very edges of the floor. Henry Lake's boiled soup smell was strong up there too, but the space was massive, the whole width of that massive house. I'd never had so much space in my life. I explored a bit, poked around in its dark corners, tried to picture it all cleaned up and perfect, but the dust in there was threatening to kill me, so I took my book, made my exit, and climbed up through the skylight and down onto the flat roof below.

I was shielded by trees up there, kind of hidden, with a view of the street in front and the sea behind. I sat with my back against the wall. Warm bricks, salt breeze, sunshine. I took some pictures of the sky on my half-dead phone. Through the cracked screen it looked like someone had taken a hammer to the clouds. The sun was bleeding rainbows round their edges. Way above all the mess and the action, the world is forever a beautiful place. I read for a bit but my head was too crowded, so I shut my eyes and let the light push through my eyelids, coral and warm. Henry's open window offered up some weird record, grown men singing through their noses, moaning all together like ten types of wind trapped down a well. There was a cricket match playing on someone's radio, the low bellow of the docks, the muted crash and roll of all that water, and above me, when I opened my eyes again and looked up, the long straight out-breath of a passing plane in the blue.

The breeze dropped. I looked down sideways over the edge of my roof to the floor below. The straw-yellow bird was dancing about on Henry's window ledge, the gulls on next door's roof sizing it up, deciding just how and when to rip it to pieces and fight over the spoils. I waved my arms at them, international bird-speak for *leave the little one alone*, and they stood up, flapped, and shifted, flinging their eyes at me like stones.

"Parker?" Henry said. "Charlie Parker, come inside at once," and it struck me, because the bird I'd always imagined Charlie Parker to be was something sleek and soaring like his music, not a fluffed-up, crapped-out old parakeet in a cage. I wondered if this Charlie Parker was even a tiny bit tempted to risk it, take its chances with the big world, and just fly. But birds like that don't survive in the wild. Not here anyway. Maybe it traveled like Henry Lake did, not for real, just in its own head. Henry's hand came out then and the bird hopped straight onto the bowl of his crumpled, ancient palm, and there was my answer. The window rumbled shut and I thought, *Oh well, we're here now, let's see what happens. I bet it's nothing at all.*

Just how wrong can a person be?

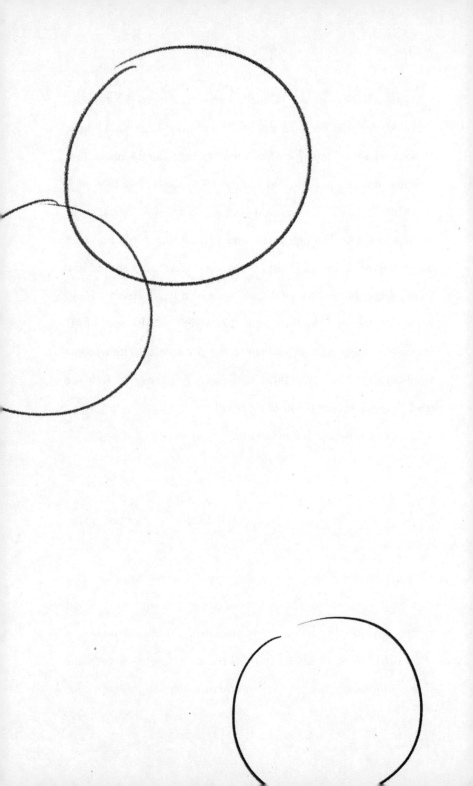

Novo

You are the place I return to, in between times. My fulcrum, the point at my center, around which all of me turns. You are my chance at stillness. The rock in my water. I know you.

I wait for you to see me. I hope for it, that pin drop in my infinities. I know to hope, but not to be certain. It is never guaranteed.

I would show you all the magic there is if you asked me. I would bring you the universe on a plate, take you out from under the rules that apply, so that anything was possible. You could slip between layers of sky and count the atoms. You could reflect light like the moon. You could hear all the languages of the world, all their words and all the wordless ones too, and you would know them. You could fly in water and swim in air.

You could spend a whole life's worth of time in the moments it takes you to blink.

I would give you anything you asked for, in exchange for one of your looks.

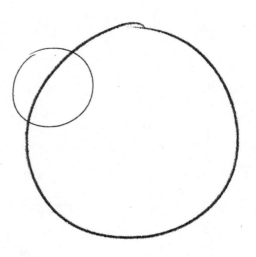

EIGHT

Jude

I remember everything about the next day clear as glass, because it's when Novo showed up. Nine thirty-four A.M. on the first of July is a page-corner, red-letter, highlighter-pen kind of Now. After it, nothing was, or is, or could ever possibly be the same. Nine thirty-three I was out front, reading in a sunlit patch of grass, medicating my sad situation with something made-up and far more dramatic, with better characters and sharper dialogue than my little life could ever muster, up until then. This thing happening, his car arriving, made me stop. Nine thirty-three was the quiet before the storm, the lull before the penny dropped, the last in-breath of life, as I knew it anyway. And then the miracle. Then Novo. I remember.

Out of nowhere, his battered black car banked the corner,

shadowing the curb like a whale underwater, swallowing up the light. A trash truck was in the road, jaws grinding, and the whale-black car had to wait behind it, stuck there for me to study, covered in dents and scrapes, engine running, windows up, music loud on the inside, I could just tell. A boy. One hand on the wheel, one arm stretched long across the blood-red leather seat-top like the branch of a tree. He bit his lip, stroked his jaw with the flat of his hand. Straightaway I wanted to be in that car with him. It pulled at me, the way you feel a tooth being pulled, not just there in your mouth, but also somehow dead center in the hub of the wheel of your stomach. I don't think I could have looked away if I'd tried, like he was the target and I was the missile—preprogrammed, set on lock, already hurtling.

He stopped across the street, outside Mrs. Midler's. Louder music, door slam, and the car dipped and sighed, missing him already as he climbed out, tall with black hair and dark clothes, a streak of ink against the blotting-paper day. He checked his watch. He stretched his arms over his head and then spread them wide, open-handed, filling the space around him, eating it up like he was hungry. He looked up at the house, touched his fingers to his mouth, a habit I would come to know so well, and that first time there was nothing else in the world suddenly, for me, only those fingers and that mouth, only him doing that. Fast and strong as a big cat he stepped onto the bonnet and then the roof of his car and took in the view, turning a slow circle, stretching again like you do after a long sleep, rolling his shoulders, arching his back. The early sun glowed warm on his skin, carved out in light and sharp shadows the wide slope of his shoulders, his collarbones, the hollows at the base of his throat. The noise of his weight on the metal sat low in the air like a gong. Wild. Unparalleled. Shining.

He jumped down and then climbed the flat front of Mrs. Midler's house, blatant, lizard-quick, balancing on the narrow ledge of an upstairs window, moving with the casual elegance of the high wire, like he was inches from the ground, not two whole floors. This boy was not afraid of falling. And he wasn't worried about getting caught either. I'd never seen anyone who cared less about that.

It was from up there that he saw me. He looked down at me and for a moment everything about him stopped, the way an animal stops when it knows it's been seen—so completely still that it hums with it, at some secret frequency, some planetary resonance, like a struck fork. Then it was over, so fast that I questioned it had happened at all. I don't think I moved either. I didn't blink. I must have stopped breathing, because it came to me from somewhere that I was running out of air. I wasn't the only one. Every other creature in striking distance forgot what they were doing for a moment when Novo landed, derailed themselves mid-train-of-thought without knowing why. I guarantee. His brazen newness brought its own brand of silence with it. Someone's cat broke from washing in a patch of sunlight, triangular, limbs stretched, feet splayed, eyes narrowed to slits. Even the gulls stopped their jaw and their hustle. It was only after he dropped neatly through an upstairs window and out of sight that the ordinary noise of things flooded back. My lungs regained their composure and the birds started up again and the cat slunk under a van and shot into a yard through a gap in the hedge. The old, always-gardening couple came out onto their porch like sleepwalkers, faces set to longing, leaf-blower to suck. The woman opposite-but-one came out and paused on her step for a second like she'd forgotten something, sniffing the air like a bloodhound, and then barricaded herself back in, kicking her door shut so hard it knocked over a plant and spoiled her spotless WELCOME mat with broken clay and clumps of thick black soil.

Upstairs, Charlie Parker was getting tangled in the curtains and I could hear Henry cursing not so quietly under his breath. Mum banged on the front window and frowned, breathing Rorschach clouds against the glass, her skin already clammy with the heat and blotched like sausage meat. I said, "Did you see that?" but she pulled a face at me, arms spread out like, *What, I have to do all this unpacking myself?* so I waved her away and pretended it wasn't anything special, even though I knew already that it was.

The mailman parked his truck at the top of the road and made his way to Mrs. Midler's front door, head down, whistle-whistle, same as usual, delivering mail to a lady who no longer existed, putting it through the letter box like nothing had changed. He didn't notice the battered black car, didn't feel all that novelty pulling on the air until it was tight as a bow. I don't know how he could have missed it.

I closed my book without bothering to mark the page, and I wondered if anyone else had heard this central thing in me, this core thing snapping like a twig. SNAP when the car pulled up and I saw that boy inside it. SNAP when we looked at each other. SNAP when those eyes blackened and that mouth opened and the breath tumbled out of him in soft clouds. He saw me watching,

I'm sure of that. We watched each other, and I still dream of it now, his body turning away like it was supposed to but his eyes staying with me, the way dancers do it, the dark and light of them the very last things to go.

NINE

I was still in my sunlit place in the yard when Novo left through his new front door, singing, and I remember thinking how brilliantly shameless that was, to exit a house you just invaded, hands in pockets, loud, like nothing-to-see-here, breezy and carefree. I recognized straight off that the rules of normal did not apply. He was untouchable. Dazzling. I imagined the force field glinting around him, all that fearlessness catching the light. And at the same time I had this feeling that he wanted me, of all people, to notice him, that he was thinking right then about me.

I hid from that feeling in the long grass because I didn't trust it. He was the width of the street away from me, and I told myself it was nothing, even though my palms felt hot and my thoughts were giddy and my heart might as well have been beating in my neck. I tried to count ordinary things—blades of grass, gravel on the path, bricks in the wall, the contents of my pockets (mostly receipts and a twisted half-pack of gum)—but none of them were ordinary enough. None of them talked me out of getting up and opening the gate. I knew straightaway that something impossible was happening, something about this boy in the world that couldn't be explained, not like a cheap magic trick anyway. I had this feeling, the kind that comes from your gut instead of your brain, the kind you should listen to, because your gut knows what it knows, and is usually right, and doesn't need anything as complicated as logic to prove it. I had this overwhelming feeling. So I followed him.

The walk to civilization from Henry Lake's house was steeply downhill, quiet, just houses, and then a right turn at the cinema onto the main road. One-way traffic, a couple of streets of shops. Less than five minutes. Not much more than ten after that to walk all the way down to the sea. The boy was fast. He moved through town the way he'd scaled that house, fluid and quick as mercury, comfortable in his own skin, happy to take up space. Everyone seemed to know him. More than that. They all wanted to welcome him, or touch him, or give him something, this returning prince, this little town's prodigal son. I'd never seen anything like it, not for real. It was more like a film set. Shopkeepers hovered in their own doorways and forced free things on him as he passed— apples, honey, bread, a bottle of wine. Fresh-caught fish. Flowers. Books. A newspaper. They competed for his attention, elbowing one another out of the way and calling after him to come and have free haircuts and tattoos, a free massage, anything he wanted from the gallery, the new collection, from their own backs. Anything at all. Children fell in behind him like ducklings, a real-life pied piper, and their parents beamed, hands clasped at their hearts, and blushed with pride. A virtual game, dreamlike, a fairy tale. As finely choreographed as a dance, seamless and elaborate, but a piece of theater all the same. It had to be. A piece of fiction. Not real. Even though I could see it unfolding right in front of me, it was somehow not real at all. A woman crossing the road held out her child for him to take, and the boy smiled and shook his head, politely declining while more children grabbed at his legs and other passersby stopped to offer him the contents of their wallets. A jeweler chased after him with a tray of watches, begging him to consider, and he took a moment to appreciate them, but he turned down those too. He walked without breaking his rhythm, weaving through the narrow lanes and around his grateful subjects as freely and elegantly as a royal breeze.

He didn't stop moving forward, didn't once look back. After he'd passed, behind him, in the space between us, those spellbound extras woke up from their dream, instantly forgot the delirium of his passing presence. The virtual went back to actual, the bright lights turned down, the extraordinary color gone. The real world zipped itself back up in his wake like water after a boat. And I saw all of it.

Down at the beach, dogs chased each other in and out of the sea. A gang of kids burrowed heads-down furiously while their parents sat in a half circle talking and staring at the waves. A pile of students played dead on blankets by the rocks. A café bustled behind where the street gave way to the sand. The boy strolled ahead of me, vivid like sunshine, and the kids looked up in unison, alert as meerkats over their castles, the talk stopped in their parents' mouths. The students stood up and drifted closer like sleepwalkers, slack-jawed with fascination, blissed out and bleary-eyed. At the edge of the water, he bent down and let his hands trail and circle, crouching low; and where he touched the sea it seemed to shimmer with phosphorescence, every cell in it lit up from within. The dogs splashed through the glimmering water, leaping and barking, surrounding him, challenging him to play. He stood up and the sea-lights flickered out. He moved backward to the line where the wet sand turns to dry, and then he sat down lead-heavy, with a sigh. The sea breathed, and he breathed, and everybody, even the dogs, went completely still. It was the loneliest thing I think I ever saw, the square root of loneliness, him sitting there with nothing moving around him at all, apart from the shifting, dimming water. Lonely warped the air around him, the way heat hangs over tarmac in the summer. It was a visible, wavering thing, clear as day. I thought I knew what lonely was until I witnessed that.

I stood there on the sand behind him, not frozen like the rest of them, immune for some reason, but still, blank with wonder, a clean slate in the shape of a person. I was trying to catch up with what was happening here. I felt as distant as Icarus suddenly, from the things I thought I knew, as far from my certain little life as that farthest single star, nine billion light-years away. The boy turned his face from the water and bit into his apple and the stilled beach started moving again. The dogs thrashed and wrestled in the waves, and the kids and their parents raised their voices in a dispute about the finer rules of their game. Amnesia swept through them like a blizzard. Nobody looked at him again. Nobody noticed. Only me.

He flattened out his newspaper to spread his gifts on it, but the wind flared, stole a page, and skipped it away toward me. As I put my foot out to stop it and pick it up, he turned. I don't remember the page number. International. Something about Yemen. Something else about a man building playgrounds in refugee camps. I do remember the look on his face though, when he saw me, as captured as those sleepwalkers, as vigilant as those kids. I was something to him. I was already, definitely something. I just knew it. We watched each other as I walked across the sand to where he was sitting in his shadow-black clothes, no more likely to keep my distance than a marble is to stay at the top of a slope.

"It's you," he said, and I said, "Yes," because what else could I say? And then I gave the page back.

He seemed to hesitate before he took it and for a moment we were both holding on to different edges of the same paper. I can't say how long that moment was, I really can't—a second, an hour, a year, they'd all work, I'd believe all of them, they could all be true.

And then I let go.

TEN

The boy lay back in the sand, and more pages cut and snapped across him in the breeze, but he didn't try to stop them. He didn't do anything. His eyes in the bright sun were black tunnels of pupil, flecks of dark and amber pressed out to the edges. I was still standing over him and I moved so his face was in my shade. The sea messed and churned behind us. I could hear its beat and pull and whisper.

One of the dogs started barking and somewhere a seagull squalled and the sand-digger kids ran toward us, around me and over him, shouting at each other, stomping down the sand, mouths open, wind stealing their words. The littlest one at the back of the group grinned at him, they grinned at each other, and as she jumped right over his body she froze, impossibly, in midair, and turned, smiling, to look straight at me. The boy lifted his arms toward her, and she caught another flying sheet of newspaper between her hands, like she was banging cymbals, and held herself still and proud in the air, still watching me, her eyes a bewitched sealskin-gray, cool and knowing. Then she landed, precise and taut as a gymnast, and her mother pounded over to collect her. "I flew," the kid said, and her mother said, "How lovely," and the boy sat back up, touched his fingers to his mouth, and watched them go.

I didn't speak. I think maybe in that moment I'd forgotten how. He held out his hand to me and I sat down next to him, silenced, and stared at the water. The old people's swimming group was bobbing about in the concrete-colored waves in their bright caps with their straight necks, like some odd species of bird. I thought, *That didn't happen, there's no way that just happened*, and I could feel him smiling then, feel him watching me. So I turned and looked at him. I had no idea what I would do next, but his smile washed over me and all I needed to do was smile back. It was that easy. An old motorbike cut through the quiet with its opened-out megaphone rattle, and up at the café someone dropped a load of plates and all the atoms of the sea crashed louder against the rocks, and the sky—that shell of atmosphere—was impossibly, ridiculously, groundbreakingly, life-changingly, earth-shatteringly blue.

ELEVEN

Memory is a distorted, persuasive thing and I can't trust it, my own version of things, but I also have to, because it's the only version I'll ever have. I think about us, me and Novo, that morning on the beach, and at first it's not so much what was said as what went on underneath that I remember best—tectonic plates moving together, a confirmation, the puzzle box sprung open. It happened fast, like everything does, and there wasn't time to think about it except there also was, enough time that while we looked at each other, I could say to myself that this was something unexpected and easy and just perfect. A run of green lights, smoothest journey ever, so you can't believe your luck and before you know it you've arrived. Alice down the rabbit hole. Edmund through the wardrobe. Us on the flattened sand, me and a tall, dark, magic, infinite boy with a quick smile and crumpled trousers and upturned palms. What did I say about the unknown? On its mark, getting set to happen. Go.

He sat close enough for me to feel the warmth of him all down my side, without touching, and while I thought about all the numberless charged particles crashing about in that slice of air between us, he asked me my name.

"Jude," I said, and he told me that *Jude the Obscure* was the saddest, bleakest book he'd ever read. "Quite a thing to have to carry around with you your whole life."

"Yeah, well," I said. "I'm just glad you're not singing the Beatles at me over and over, like everybody else does. Longest song on earth, and let's face it, not the best."

He laughed, a match strike lighting up corners of the day I hadn't even looked at.

"I'm Novo," he said, and I knew instantly that it was the only name in the history of names good enough for him.

That's when he hit me with the Saint Jude thing—patron saint of lost causes—and I was like, "Really? Why didn't I know that?" and I thought, even then, that this was bound to be one of them, a lost cause. That this was going to trample all over us whether we wanted it to or not.

"Whatever," I said. "Lost causes are underrated anyway."

He took my hand, and my skin lit up like the sea under his fingers, pulsed and shimmered just below the surface, and we both watched it, we both smiled, and I wasn't afraid, not even for the smallest fraction of a second. Not ever.

"Pleased to meet you, Novo," I said, my veins full of fireflies.

We just looked at each other, without speaking, without needing to speak, and then I broke the quiet.

"What is this?" I said, holding my arms out, still filled with light. "How do you do that?"

And even as I asked it, I knew I was in over my head.

"That's just me, being me," he said.

I nodded like I understood. But I didn't. I couldn't.

He said, "I warn you. I'm not from here."

I laughed. "Yeah. Me neither."

His eyes were black and white. "I mean I'm not from anywhere, Jude. I'm not like you. Do you understand?"

"Yes," I said. "I do. I can see that. I believe you."

The morning was golden and the air was laced at the edges with the stink of kelp and saltwater. Birds picked intently at the baking seaweed, patrolling their lines and lifting now and then straight up into the air on invisible currents.

Novo smiled and shook his head a little.

"Are you ready?" he said.

"For what?"

"For everything I have to give you."

"What do you mean?"

"You have a choice. You can say no and get up now and go back to your old life, same as it was, and nothing bad will happen. I won't bother you. I promise I won't do that."

"Or?"

"Or you can take a chance," he said. "Say yes."

"To what?"

Novo shrugged. He hadn't taken his eyes off me. Not once. "To everything."

I laughed a little, leaned back in the sand, finding the cool beneath its surface with the points of my elbows. "What's everything?"

He thought about it for a moment. "Everything possible and impossible," he said. "No distinction. I come from a place between things. Ten lifetimes of adventure on the head of a pin. Unrepeatable and unforgettable."

"Are you serious?" I said. "Do I have to say yes or no?"

"Absolutely. This is a moment," he said. "Mark it. Life changing. I guarantee."

"And what's the catch?"

"The catch?"

"Yes. What's the downside?"

He smiled at me. "We don't know that yet."

I breathed in. Like I'd pick cleaning out kitchen cupboards with my perpetually disappointed mother over this. As if.

"Well then, yes," I said.

"You're with me?" he said. "You're in?"

"Of course I'm in." Though I had no idea what that meant.

He closed his eyes for the quickest moment, and when he opened them again and looked at me, something shifted in the air around us. Maybe even the air itself. The light changed and it fell away, a veil, the finest curtain, so that I could see the paths that birds carved up and down the blue sky, count the million points of light on the water, feel the singular oneness of every grain of sand and every atom in my own body. Strong. Like we were the exact same thing.

"What's happening?" I said, and he smiled again.

"I told you. Everything. All at once."

Either I was disappearing into my surroundings or they were disappearing into me. I inhaled the whole world, drew it into me cool and clear, and then exhaled it again, letting it go, putting it back, warm with the heat of my blood, over and over again. The world was my lungs and my lungs were the sea and the sea was everywhere.

"Hello Now," Novo said, and I said, "What?" because all life was so loud in my ears suddenly, I didn't think I'd heard him right. I didn't know yet that it was the spell cast, right then, in that moment, and all the known rules thrown out. I didn't know it was the start of something wild and unforgettable, impossible and true.

"Hello Now," he said again, smiling, not just at me, but at all of it. Everything. "Oh, and look. Here's another Now. Hello to that one too."

The colors were beyond brighter. The details were infinitely sharper. Words can't work hard enough to keep up with that sudden change in the fabric of everything. I can't make them tell it right. We glowed, the two of us, sitting there. We were the whole world and we were nothing but atoms. I could feel the white heat of the sun rising right off my skin. Somewhere both other and also the same, the beach around us carried on as normal—the swimmers and surfers, the kids with their buckets, the rocks and the dogs and the wheeling gulls, the constant water. I was there too, with everyone, on the sand, and I was also elsewhere. I was the rock on the ground and the kite tied to it, stretching and flexing high up in the thin air. I was both. We were both. That's what it felt like, to me.

The world breathed and the sea breathed and we breathed. Time stretched and contracted, part light speed, part glacial, until I lost track of even losing track, and the sun, which had been barely moving in the sky, was burning suddenly low on the horizon and filling that whole stretch of water with flames. It was colder and the beach was empty and there was just us.

"You can stay inside any Now with me," Novo said. "You can stop and take your time and look around."

The wind dropped as quick as a ball and the moonless sea was ink-black and punctured with stars.

"I can't tell where it ends and begins," I said, speaking for the first time in what could have been centuries.

"Where what ends and begins?"

"Everything," I said. "I can't tell without the horizon."

"It doesn't end or begin," Novo said. "It just is." And then we stood up on the black sand and walked through the pitch-dark ghost of town, back up the hill to our houses.

TWELVE

Up the hill and right at the corner onto our street, I didn't hear anything until we were almost on top of it. The noise was trapped somehow and didn't travel, not the way noises are supposed to. Outside Mrs. Midler's, there was already too much frantic activity for me to get too close, but still, even though I could see all that was going on, there wasn't one sound. I stood back on the lawn and felt the total quiet at all its edges while the house shed its own skin. I watched as it rid itself of the stuff it didn't want— carpets, sacks of wallpaper, broken furniture, all sailing out of windows, all landing, more or less, in a massive heap out front. An orchestral sort of hum went with everything—base sander, the rhythm of hammers, the high sharp notes of screwdrivers and drills, so that it sounded like the place was filling up with giant bees. Novo moved ahead of me through the noise and the chaos to the door. I stood watching, and I thought of that film when the front of a house falls down on top of Buster Keaton in a storm and he stands up unscathed in the neat gap left by an open window. I thought of those buildings in war zones, patchworks of exposed interiors like dolls' houses, except real as can be, someone's home, and bombed inside out.

Novo turned toward me with his arms out wide, the orchestra's conductor. Behind him, the windows rattled and a sofa launched itself into the air and landed on the grass with a shudder.

"Do you like what I'm doing with the place?" he yelled, and his half-drowned-out voice sounded like it was coming from streets away. I could only just about hear it.

I was still at the end of the yard, right at the line between this impossible building site and total quiet. Moving my head, even just a little, took me from silence to commotion and back again. All the lights in the other houses were out, all the streetlamps too. For a second I thought there was a flicker of something at our place, at Henry's, a blown-out candle maybe, a lighter flame, but when I looked over it was dark, same as the rest of them, so I couldn't be sure of what I'd seen. I couldn't be sure of anything, come to think of it.

"Can you explain though?" I said as six chairs marched through the front window and onto the lawn. "Please? I mean, to me?"

"Is it wearing off?" he said.

"Is what wearing off?" I said, and I ran through my list of known hallucinogens: acid, mushrooms, mescaline, DMT, ket, PCP.

"What is it?" I said. "Which one have I taken?"

"Stop," he said. "Jude. You haven't taken anything. I just softened the border, that's all."

"What border?"

"Between us. So you can see what I see, without losing it."

"I am losing it though," I said. "I really think I might be."

He walked across the dark lawn and put his hands on my shoulders, like I was a lighter-than-air thing, a thing that needed holding down. The glow from his hands fell through me like a faraway firework.

"How is this possible?" I said, and Novo stretched his arms above his head and licked his lips and smiled at me.

"Anything is. I told you. Just breathe, Jude. It's all good. You can trust me."

He pulled us both out of the noise, into the sleeping street, and he put his finger to his lips, his soft sigh lifting the stooped flowers, stirring the leaves high in the trees.

"Are you real?" I asked him, and he smiled.

"I don't know. Are you?"

"Am I dreaming?" I said. "Are we in a dream?"

"Maybe. Probably. What would you do if we were?"

I knew the answer instantly, felt it without thinking, a stone in my belly, how pockmarked with letdowns the rest of my life was going to be if I woke up. I knew all this, and more, even though we'd only just met.

"That's easy," I told him. "I'd just stay asleep."

THIRTEEN

Time all but stopped when Novo and I were together. The afternoon I followed him through town to the beach, whole days passed inside the world we created. But back at our house, at Henry Lake's house, time had hardly moved. Mum was on her way down the stairs when I opened the front door, and she just about registered my presence, as if she'd knocked on her bedroom window and frowned at me in the yard seconds before, as if that had only just finished happening. She still wasn't dressed. She didn't see Novo because he stayed back, behind me. I felt him hold back. I felt him pause.

"Coffee?" she said, and I said, "Not for me," and she carried on into the kitchen, her slippers face-slapping the floorboards all the way. I heard her slamming cupboard doors and banging stuff down on the counter, crashing through still-packed boxes to find the coffeepot. A one-woman symphony of rage. I didn't know what it was this time. There was always something. Like it was just built in. My mum never closed a door if she could slam it. She stomped when she walked, like she was crushing bugs. She held things like she wanted more than anything to break them. She shouted, even when she said she wasn't angry. She'd done it since I was born, as far as I could make out. She probably did it before. My earliest memory is of her playing a room like a set of drums, bashing out rhythms with the sheer force of her disappointment and fury, and who knows? That might even have been when I was still in the womb.

Novo stepped inside and stood next to me in the hallway. I took his hand and we started up the stairs. Henry's door was shut as we passed it on the landing. I told Novo not to expect much. "We only just moved in, remember. I've hardly touched it," but the room we walked into was completely different. Not full of dust and dead flies. Not unclaimed and empty at all. The floorboards and walls were a clean bright white and covered already with my rugs and posters. My bed was in the corner under the skylight, my books were unpacked and on shelves. There were plants and candles, an angled lamp and a slender wooden rocking chair I'd only ever seen in the pages of a magazine. It was the room I didn't know I'd been imagining for years.

"Who did this?" I said, and Novo smiled.

"This was you?"

He shrugged. "It did itself, really. Same as mine."

"It did itself."

"Is it okay? Do you like it?"

"It's perfect," I said, pulling at drawers, scanning my bookshelf, opening the wardrobe. Everything was where it should be. Some of it was mine and some was brand-new but I also knew it, knew where everything was supposed to be, like I'd done it myself. I remember wondering if Novo could see inside me, see my imagination like a film screen, and I didn't want to know the answer. I didn't even want to ask.

"Am I scaring you?" he said.

It was ridiculous and unthinkable. It should have scared me. But what can I say? It just didn't.

"I mean. This is nothing," he said. "A bit of DIY. If this was too much already then we'd have a problem."

I smiled at him. "You're not scaring me."

"Good," he said, looking up through the skylight. "That's good."

"Want to see the roof?" I said, standing on the bed and pulling myself up and through it. Novo came up after me and we stood together outside under that dome of blue. Down below us, across the street, the noise had finished now and all the contents of Mrs. Midler's house were in the front yard, arranged room by room, as if the building had just picked itself up and moved over a bit when our backs were turned. There were people out there, milling about, picking over everything. Two women in bright anoraks were having a serious think about some hunting-scene place mats. Some kids played building blocks with a load of shell-thin china cups until somebody noticed and told them to stop. A man was trying to persuade his wife to take home an enormous oil painting of a dog. The woman opposite-but-one was looking at lamps, tugging at their wiring, lifting them up to see underneath. Other strangers flicked mercilessly through Mrs. Midler's books, pulled at her clothes with the tips of their fingers, passed judgment on her taste in art and crammed their feet into her favorite shoes. A girl at a table full of jewelry weighed a pair of heavy costume earrings in her hand.

I thought about Mrs. Midler's life, whoever she was. Unique, same as everyone else's, with its own bar charts of disappointment and reward, its own strict and arbitrary rules. And still somehow it ended up in boxes marked HELP YOURSELF.

"It's her life story," Novo said, and I said, "Yes. I was thinking that. Let's go down there. I'd like to see."

So we did, and I found myself standing at a table packed sky-high with matching china. An obstacle course of etiquette broken up into affordable lots, so the soup bowls would never again see the saucers, the breakfast cups the milk jug. Nobody likes being dismantled. Nothing wants to get taken apart. I felt sorry for them, even if they were only plates.

Novo picked up a cup and the pattern on it glowed, almost fluorescent. His touch changed the chemical composition of everything, trailing technicolor, the space around him so much bolder and more vivid than anywhere else. He blinked slowly. All over the garden people stretched like cats and curled back into themselves, suddenly blissful, practically purring. It was as if he'd dropped a euphoric in the tap water. Faces soft as warm butter, the hard locks suddenly gone from jaws, scowls smoothed out like they were pillowcases and Novo was the iron. The woman opposite-but-one, so tightly wound, went all out of character, loose-limbed and agile, and swept like a dancer across the lawn. The knotty old couple glowed and stippled like sunlight in a forest. This little boy was screaming in his stroller and when Novo smiled at him the screaming stopped, just like that, and the boy went straight to sleep, thumb-in-mouth blissful. I wondered if anybody noticed it on me—my right smile back, my long spine, this warm-bath feel, the way everything was precisely and fluidly and perfectly itself, because of him.

He turned in a circle, and everyone in the garden turned too, exactly the same but just a beat behind him, like an echo. I saw it.

"Shall we have some fun?" he said.

"Always."

He laughed. "Can you dance?"

"Maybe."

"I bet you're good," he said.

"You reckon?"

"Sure. But are you as good as *us*?"

He was smiling, lifting his arms over his head, tilting his chin while all around, the assembled company copied him and lifted theirs. He turned again, a slower circle, arms out, palms flat, graceful as a dervish, and every single person on that lawn did the same. It was a natural, peaceful thing to watch, like a cornfield bowing in a breeze, or the stop-frame blooming of a rose. If

Novo was the stone hitting the water, the people all around us were the ripple.

"Let's see," he said, and he stepped close to me and slipped his arm round my waist, and for a second, all of my thoughts were focused right there, only there, where he was touching me. All over the garden, people reached for one another the way we did, and stood joined and waiting.

"Ready?" Novo said, and his cheek was as close as it could be to mine without actually touching, and I felt the soft warmth of his skin near mine, and he took my hand.

Music started up somewhere. The piano was playing itself, and the kids with the china cups were on percussion, a yard-sale orchestra, cutlery and plates, doorstops and old telephones chinking and clattering in perfect time, an odd and delicate, off-kilter, handmade sound. Novo and I spun, and the garden spun, and even with my eyes wide open this was suddenly not a Saturday-morning house-clearance giveaway at all, but some kind of extravagant masked ball, rich with elaborate costume, the sky over our heads heavy with sparkling chandeliers. Bright anoraks became cloaks, and the women in them poured champagne out of watering cans. The knotty old couple glinted with diamonds. Mrs. Midler's earrings caught the light as the girl wearing them leaned in closely to her partner and poured her smile into his eyes and lifted her chin to laugh. Novo held on to me and we turned with the crowd in the garden in ever-tightening rounds, the air bristling with the sweep and whisper of gowns, the flattened grass sighing, the dance pulling more and more of the world into itself like a whirlpool, quicker and quicker, snapshot and time travel and film set, until what began as a slow circle got spun out and ramped up, feverish and chaotic.

Novo turned me and turned me and that was when I saw Henry Lake at his window, watching. He was rooted to the spot, the only piece of stillness in that whirlpool, the only one of all of us and everything that wasn't moving. I looked for him again as we spun and there he was, and a third time, and a fourth. A statue leaning out into the air, his face a dull stone, his mouth open, his startled eyes.

"Wait," I said to Novo.

"Too much?" he said. "Too Cinderella maybe?" and the music changed suddenly to something distorted and industrial, something played on vacuum and food processor and megaphone and iron poker. Berlin nightclub, the sky low and solid as a ceiling, and the crowd changed suddenly, cornered and edgy, closing in, drawing together, hot with effort, claustrophobic, breathless, sweating. Their eyes looked like Charlie Parker's eyes—quick black buttons, all reflective, absorbing nothing. I shook my head. "Stop."

Novo stopped instantly and closed his eyes, and when he inhaled I felt my own lungs expand too. The yard went silent, holding itself at the top of his breath, and a cloud went over the sun so that everything was gray for less than a second, and steel-cold, like a blade. Then the blade flashed, Novo breathed out, and the world went back to what it was before. All the bargain hunters picked up where they left off—trawling through cutlery, sniffing the armpits of coats, counting out change, like nothing out of the ordinary had ever happened. All except Henry, a gargoyle at his window, his eyes the only part of him quick and alive, fixed on Novo, all recognition and devotion but also something more. Something darker. Something like pain. Or fear. I pointed up at him, "Look," and I held Novo's arms and turned him slightly, in the right direction, so he could see.

For a moment he was as still as Henry. The two of them were the same cold column of stone. Everything else inside that moment was still too, the crowd under his spell and also the circling birds and the ants all-day-long seething in the pavement cracks and the nodding flower heads and the leaves that should have been shivering in the breeze.

Even the breeze.

Everything stopped. And, where time is anything but linear, I think there's a place, in or out of the known universe, where that is still happening, where Henry and Novo are still seeing each other for the first time in a garden full of spellbound strangers and a dead old lady's things, with me as their witness. And what I'm witnessing is strong enough to bring life itself to a halt.

Novo moved first. Nothing else. He said something under his breath, like "Unbelievable," and his searchlight eyes turned on me. I felt his fingers, light as feathers, on my arm.

"Do you know that man in your house?" he said.

"Yes."

"Who is he? Not family?"

"No. He was already there. Kind of part of the deal. It's Henry."

"Henry," he said. "*Henry*," and he opened his arms then, high and wide, in something like triumph, and with my own eyes I saw Henry Lake's weightless body float straight through the window and out into the paralyzed air in bewildered slow motion, moving more like a strung puppet than a man. He got closer, limbs flailing, until he was hovering just above us, his mouth clamped shut, his eyes burning white-hot with the things he wanted desperately to say.

"What are you doing?" I said to Novo, but he didn't answer. "Why are you doing that to him?"

Tears welled up in Henry's eyes and fell on my face like the beginnings of rain, and his mouth bubbled and trembled like a saucepan lid, and in the corner of the sky I caught a fork of white lightning and I counted to four before the thunder growled.

I looked at Novo, and I was so ready to call him cruel, so close to getting it wrong, but his eyes were full of tears too, so I bit my tongue, and held still, and just watched. He steadied himself to guide Henry down, and the old man landed lightly in his arms. So insubstantial and frail, hardly more than a heap of clothing. His panic vanished. He rested his head on Novo's shoulder like a child, and Novo folded over him, a bird in sleep, and they were quiet, and they glowed like soft bulbs, there on the stopped lawn, their heads together, just touching. They made a circuit, and the current that passed through them was silent and lit with bliss.

I don't know how long it lasted. I got lost just watching. Even to see it was the prize. When it was over, Novo opened his eyes, and in the time it took for him to blink the world sprang forward, catching up with itself like a piece of pulled elastic, stretched tight to its absolute limit and then let go—the birds circling, the ants seething, the nodding flowers and shivering leaves. Henry was at his window again, order restored, curtains fluttering, Charlie Parker hopping on the sill. He and Novo were still watching each other but there was no hint of cold stone anymore. All I could see in the air between them was a trace of hot light, fine as thread, and glinting like fire.

Novo reached for my hand again and held on to it, and my veins ran with warm honey. He laughed softly to himself and shook his head slowly from side to side, one hand still on mine, the other cradling his own cheek. He didn't speak.

"Novo," I said. "What just happened?"

Quick pulses of light still surged beneath his skin. The look on his face said he'd just seen a miracle, this miracle boy. I remember thinking that must mean there are infinite levels of wonder, like a never-ending staircase, so that everyone gets to look up at something like that, whoever they are, and I really hoped I was onto something. I really wanted to be right.

Novo hadn't spoken. "Can't you tell me?" I said, and he shook his head and his voice was soft and quiet when he said, "Not yet."

Under the high sun, his shadow was pure light. He was the magnifying glass, focusing the heat onto pinpoints of ground that simmered and caught behind him. The same pure light was coming from where Henry stood, billowing out into the morning in clouds of dazzle and luminous smoke. Novo picked me up suddenly and swung me around so the rest of the garden was a blur of color. He was a disco ball on the ceiling, setting off quick bouncing sparks of fire all around us. When he put me down, the light pouring from Henry's window began to splutter and fade, faintly at first and then with gathering speed. I could still see the bright thread, but the thick clouds were diffusing into the sky, a paintbrush dipped in water.

I pictured the Henry I'd met, stuck in those rooms with that dodgy bird and that rank soup and that rickety old laptop, pretending to travel. How could an old man like that have such an impact on this boy?

Novo was still looking up at him.

"What are you thinking?" I said.

"I'm wondering what I can do. I'm hoping he's all right."

"He never leaves the house," I said. "I mean, *never.*"

"No. He can't."

"Oh, you knew that already?"

He smiled. "I'm not even sure."

All the people in the garden, helping themselves to things,

and not one of them looked up and saw the thread of light, those brilliant, fading clouds. Not one of them noticed the tiny fires that peppered the lawn. It's staggering, the things we miss when we're not searching for them, but facing the wrong direction, looking down.

"Am I the only one who can see this?" I said, and Novo looked at me then, his arms still round my waist.

"Yes, Jude," he said. "You are the only one."

He moved and his shadow moved and the tiny fires followed. They burned a hole in one of Mrs. Midler's evening dresses. They ate through someone's raincoat, the plastic blistering and puckering in the heat.

"You're setting fire to everything," I said. "Look."

"Am I?" he said.

The garden began to empty around us, people drifting away with their new junk, the party suddenly over. Upstairs, Henry's window rattled shut.

Novo said, "I'd like to check on him. Let's go back inside," and the glow in him faded too. All the fires went out at once and his shadow went back to what it should have been, same as everyone else's, just an absence of light.

FOURTEEN

The house was dead quiet and we filled it with sound. Our steps on the floorboards, the creak of us on the stairs. Novo breathing, a seashell sound, in and out, soft and constant. I could hear Henry's ticking clocks. His door was wide open for a change, bright sunlight streaming onto the landing in strong, straight lines like someone had marked it there with a ruler.

He was feeding the gulls. Three of them clashed and wheeled outside his window—wild and powerful that close up, their wide wingspan, their sharp, watchful heads.

"Henry?" Novo said.

He didn't turn round. "Come in, both of you. Come in."

Charlie Parker tried to fly through the walls when we went in there, went at it like a fly at a window, wings hammering away.

"It's okay," Henry said. "It's okay, Charlie. Calm down."

I looked at Novo. I asked him, without speaking, what that was about, and without speaking, he said he didn't know. We watched as Charlie Parker panicked and Henry made clicking noises and held a thin strip of fish out the window. One of the birds angled sharply in the glare and snatched it out of his hand with its precise beak. The pins on the big map of the world glinted in the bright light.

"Don't be scared of him, Jude," Henry said. "He won't hurt you." And I couldn't say then, in that moment, if he meant the feeding bird or Novo.

"I'm not scared. I'm not scared of him at all."

"I've known these gulls since they were young," Henry said. "I knew their parents and their grandparents. Every year they come and visit. I can tell by their markings. The red spot on this one's beak. That one's mottled wing. They are seven or eight now. Did you know that seagulls can live to be fifteen?"

I shook my head. "No," I said. "I didn't."

"It's in their nature to come back," Henry said. "Even a caged bird turns like a compass when the time comes. And it's in my nature to stay here and wait."

Novo still hadn't spoken. He was watching Henry so carefully, with so much focus, same as the seagulls at the window. They cut and hovered at a distance, responding to his every move, the exact same height in the sky as his bony, outstretched arm. They cut and hovered, and Novo watched, and it seemed like nothing else in the world was happening that was more important than that.

I had so many questions. I could feel it, the current of the unsaid, circling the room, that thread of light between them still there somehow, still glinting. I wanted to try to understand what was going on. But Henry Lake turned before I could speak, his back to the light, his face in darkness, shielded again, all hat and beard and dark glasses. He took the glasses off and he and Novo looked at each other for a long time, and there was no speaking then. There was no breaking into that. Charlie Parker landed soundlessly on the table and settled down. Henry looked up at the painting of the dark-haired woman, her beautiful back, that tantalizing almost-turn.

"Is that her?" Novo said, and I said, "Who?" and Henry smiled. "Yes."

"Who is she?" I said, and Novo said, "She's beautiful."

"Her name was Dulcie," Henry said, and for a second the lights flickered under his skin, the way I'd seen my own skin shimmer, and his eyes filled instantly with tears.

"You?" I said to him. "You too?" But Henry said nothing, he just sat there, glowing and weeping.

"What is it, Henry?" I said. "Novo. What does he know?"

"I loved her," Henry said, still looking up at her, still waiting, as if she might turn at any moment.

"When?" Novo asked. "How long?" and Henry sighed. "A moment. A lifetime ago. A whole lifetime."

He looked away and wiped his eyes. "There was never enough time," he said.

"For what?" I said, and that look passed between them again, all the things they knew and I didn't. "What's happening?"

"We have time now," Novo said, sitting down on the sofa, pulling me toward him.

"But that's *your* time," Henry said. "You shouldn't waste it on me."

"Jude needs to know," he said. "Do it for Jude."

I had no idea what that meant, but I leaned into Novo and he put his arm around me, and Henry watched us. He smiled.

"Tell us about her," Novo said. "Tell us Dulcie's story. Come on. You know as well as I do that right now we have all the time in the world."

FIFTEEN

Henry sat down, and Charlie Parker hopped onto the back of the chair, just behind him. Downstairs a door banged shut and another one groaned open and then it was pin-drop quiet while we waited for him to begin.

"There are so many doors between this life and my last," Henry finally said, and Novo smiled.

"I could never remember them all."

"It doesn't matter how many," Novo said.

"No. Just what's on the other side," Henry said, and his skin flickered again, and his eyes lit up. "I saw her first. Dulcie. I knew her before I met her. I think I always knew. But still. I was blindsided."

"Where did you meet her?" I asked him.

"The first time? On a boat," he said. "We were on a boat. There was a terrible storm. Forty of us, maybe more, trapped like cattle on our way to the slaughter, showing the whites of our eyes."

"When was this?" I said.

"I was about your age. I was practically brand-new. I remember the horizon. Blue on blue, and nothing else, in a fine, straight line. I let myself stretch out along it. I made my mind wire-thin."

I thought of the moment, only hours ago, on the dark beach when I couldn't tell them apart, the sky and the sea.

"The edge of things," Novo was saying. "The line between."

"I couldn't think how far away it was, as far as the eye could see, and afterward I learned the equation by heart: $1.22459\sqrt{h}$, where h is the height above sea level. The distance that first time was about four miles. But the line itself is endless."

"Yes," Novo said.

Henry narrowed his eyes as if he could still see it. "Sun on its decks, all that red metal crusted with rust and bird shit. The sky above us was thick with gulls. There was no sign of the storm."

He bowed his head. "When all around you is water, and all you can hear and smell and feel is the boom and stench and weight of water throwing itself against you, you forget everything."

Novo reached out and took his hand, and that's when I felt it, this dank, dead cold lapping at my ankles, and when I looked down, the floor was moving, soupy with murk and bird droppings and the glinting scraps of dead fish, like the bottom of a boat.

"What's happening?" I said, and Novo's grip tightened on Henry Lake's hand.

"Just a memory," he said, his other arm still round me. "Not real. Not now. I promise."

He closed his eyes but I kept mine open while the whole room peaked and dropped on those remembered waves, over and over, the walls outside battered by great punching gusts of wind, the rain that landed on the windows deafening and relentless. I watched it all.

"Only two things were sure in that moment," Henry said. "My death and the water. I tried to picture the world without me and it was easy. I knew the world wouldn't notice. I wondered if there was anyone on that boat the world would miss. I thought about them all dying and their families never knowing, only picturing them alive and well, and if that would make a difference, if that would keep a part of them alive and well somewhere after all."

"I've thought that," Novo said. "I've wondered that."

"And then I saw her," Henry said. "The woman next to me was

trying to comfort her daughter. The little girl screamed with each drop of the wave, screamed with everything she had. I could see the white arcs of her teeth and the back of her throat, but I could hardly hear her over the noise. And then she lifted her head and looked at me."

"The woman?"

"No. The girl. She looked at me and her eyes saw everything. With the movement of the waves, the high sky, and the dark slap of the water, she was there and then gone, there and then gone. But still, she anchored me to something. Just the sight of her stilled that storm, for me."

"Yes," Novo said. "That's it."

That thread between them again, turning and glinting. A secret understanding. The look they shared keeping me out.

The storm in the room dropped. The waves of Henry's memory flattened out. The water at our feet went still, like dirty glass.

"And then?" I said.

Henry said, "She asked her mother, 'Are we dead?' and I could see in her eyes that the woman wasn't sure when she told her daughter, 'No.' I looked away from her for half a second. Less. And when I looked back, she was gone."

"Gone?" I said. "How could she be gone?"

Henry shrugged. "I couldn't find her," he told me as the water drained through the floorboards, leaving dirty great marks on the walls and the skirting boards. I pictured Mum downstairs, seawater raining down on her in her new kitchen. I half expected to hear her call out, but she didn't. The rest of the house was silent. The sky outside was blue and still. There wasn't a leaf moving on the trees.

Novo let go of Henry's hand. "And after that?" he said. "The next time?"

"It was here. I saw the back of her, going into this house. She was older. But I knew her instantly. I would have known her anywhere."

The memory glowed on his face, warm as the sun on a bright wall. We all felt it. Henry closed his eyes again. "She went in and left the door open, and I tried to see something more in that brief slice of inside, but there was nothing there for me to see, just her disappearing into the dark. She looked like she was stepping out of one world and into another. I knew even then that before long I would go in, that a part of me already had."

"So when did you?" I said.

"Not right away. I walked past, every day, for weeks, but the house looked so shut up and abandoned. I started to lose hope.

And then, one day, there she was, at an upstairs window. This window, in fact." He pointed. "This one right here."

"And what happened?" Novo said.

"Well. I stopped. And I waved at her. And she went very still, as if she didn't want to be seen at all."

"Like you did," I said to Novo. "Just like you did," and he smiled.

"My heart went into a tailspin in my chest," Henry said.

"And then?"

"And then," he said, "she smiled. She ran downstairs and opened the door. And my heart righted itself and flew straight. I stood at the gate and she stepped out barefoot onto the path. She was wearing a thin black dress and an old black robe, and her hair was black and her skin was the color of honey. I hadn't opened the gate yet. I hadn't moved.

"'Aren't you coming in?' she said. Just like that. I walked up that path and I took off my boots before I followed her in. It seemed like the polite thing to do. Outside I could hear sounds, birdsong and wing flap, a light wind in the trees, a passing car. Inside was silent. As if the house was holding its breath. She was already at the top of the stairs, smiling. She held her hands out toward me."

Henry's smile was bright with rapture, lost in the story that was so long ago and could be yesterday, could still be happening right now, for him.

"Did she recognize you?" Novo said.

He nodded. "She couldn't think where from. I didn't tell her about the boat. Not at first. I didn't want to make her remember."

"But you told her later," I said.

"Yes. Of course. In the end, I told her everything."

"Tell us about her," Novo said, and I could see from his face that he was as bewitched by this story as Henry. That it was the stuff of legend now, for him.

Henry sighed. "Everything about her was spectacular. I remember watching her throw a ball into the sky until it disappeared. I remember her careering down the hill from the top of town on a cart she'd made from fruit boxes and an old stroller, heading straight for a tree, swerving at the last minute. I would have sworn an oath that the cart took off. I was utterly convinced that she flew. Dulcie was fearless. She really lived. She did everything better and everything first, before me.

"The morning after I found her, I woke up in a clean bed in a bright room. I felt alive, for the first time I could remember. I came downstairs to find her and she was in the yard. She didn't look at me. But she always knew when I was there just the same.

"She had a huge kite and she was untangling the string. She said, 'Hold this, and don't move,' and I held it and every muscle in my body as still as stone for fear of disappointing her. The smile stayed locked on my face, like rigor mortis, like a happy corpse. I did exactly as she asked, and Dulcie liked that. When she had finished untying the knots, she let me come with her to fly it—to watch while she flew it, at least. I can still feel the ache in my neck from looking up as it turned on the wind, free as a bird and still tied to her, the strings invisible, so it looked like it was just her deft hands anchoring it, strong and heavy, to the ground. For days afterward, I kept seeing her hands, and the look on her face, and the kite whipping and spinning above her. Pure magic." He smiled. "Pure magic."

He got up and went to a drawer in his bedroom and pulled out a box. His feet shuffled on the floorboards like they were tied together at the ankles. Such slow, small steps. He brought the box back to us and opened it and filled our hands with old photos, some black and white, some color, paled with age. The woman from the painting, her whole face, her wide smile. And Henry. Young and dark and clean-shaven, with fierce eyes. He hardly registered the camera. He was almost always looking at her.

Novo was quiet, and ran his fingers over their faces, and frowned.

"After that, we were never apart," Henry said.

"Really?" I said.

He blinked. "Not once." Then he looked at Novo and said, "Please. Can I see us?" and when Novo nodded, the bright room went dark, and Henry's memory played out in front of us like old film, soft at the edges, scratched and jumpy. Dulcie, larger than life and sheer as a ghost, graceful and smiling, reached out from some ephemeral half-place for Henry's hands, and part of him watched with us while another seemed to move before our eyes with the strength and power of his younger self, sweeping Dulcie off the ground, her black skirts turning in a circle, her bare feet. Images crowded the room in hologram layers, a chaotic slideshow. Her head on his shoulder. Their joined hands. A face in close fragments—the corner of her mouth, a tiny scar by her eye. A walk in the long grass. Stone beach by a river. The flat sea rolling from the deck of a ship. Cities and deserts. Mountains and palaces and canyons. Countless memories, speeded to a blur like the moving blades of a fan, passed over us like whipped air. And then, lastly, rooms in a house, this house, different but familiar. A painted chair. And Dulcie, sitting up in bed now, thinner, older, smiling at us all with a world of sadness spinning in her eyes.

She faded slowly, and then the room was bright again, the window open, the seagulls calling for Henry, crying for more.

"She always wore black," Henry said. "Every day of her life. Black dresses. A black robe. Her wardrobe was like a funeral parlor. Look."

He unlocked one of the giant wardrobes taking up space against the wall, and it jostled with the swing of black skirts— silk and wool and organza and lace. Elaborate and old-fashioned, they smelled of mothballs, and Henry ran his hand across them like a pianist, and bowed his head and closed the doors.

"What happened to her?" I said.

He gave a sad smile. "She died, Jude. She lived and we were happy together and there was a lifetime in each heartbeat, a million perfect Nows. And then she died."

"I'm so sorry."

He looked at Novo. "It was a long time ago."

"And you've been here ever since?"

Henry nodded.

"I kept everything," he said. "At the beginning, I was sure she would come back. I couldn't understand it, not really. I pictured her rushing in the front door and scolding me for getting rid of all her things."

I thought of Mrs. Midler's life laid out like that, the flesh picked off its bones, those plates, split apart like orphaned children.

"Later," he said, "when I knew she wasn't ever coming back, when I finally understood her death for what it was, as something permanent, I just couldn't bear to part with them."

"What else was hers?" I said.

"The clocks. All the furniture. Those books. The map of the world. Dulcie loved to travel." He looked at the map and at us, and he wiped his watery eyes, pale as marble. "But after she left, I never could."

Novo put his hand on me, and I looked down, and I held it in both of mine, his skin its own map, his body another country.

Henry got up and walked to the window. The sun shone almost straight through him, like he was made of paper, or something thinner than flesh. He took a long, deep breath, and he was shaking a little.

"Are you okay?" I said.

He bowed his head, under the weight of it, and the pulse in my veins got bass heavy, and my heart felt huge in my chest. "The next part has been hard."

"Stop now," Novo said. "Take a rest. You're exhausted."

Henry looked at him, and I knew there was something else they weren't saying then, to me.

"What is it, Henry?" I said.

"Nothing compares," he said. "Nowhere near. Never will."

"Compares to what?" I said, and Henry didn't speak for a minute. He held one more piece of fish out for the birds and then he wiped his hand on a rag and went over to the chair where Charlie Parker was still perched. He stroked the bird's tired feathers with one gentle finger, took off his glasses, and brought it up to his face for a closer look, his pale eyes flat with sadness, his frown a deep dark line.

"To this," Novo told me, taking my hand, bringing my knuckles to his cheek, holding it there. "Nothing compares to us."

SIXTEEN

We scaled the wall at the side of the house, up to my roof, Novo and I. I climbed up first so I could watch him arrive: hands first, then face and eyes and shoulders. We looked at each other, for too long, without speaking. I remember thinking if I looked away he might fall and I'd be to blame, like I was the only thing keeping him up there. There's not much I wouldn't give to have that over again, that feeling at the beginning, whatever the risks. He crouched there, a hand's width from me, and it was like seeing him through a microscope or something, so much detail, like I had nothing else to look at in the world. Only him. Nothing but him. Tiny scar on his cheekbone, hairline crack in his tooth, and his mouth—soft, I already knew it, and dark as a bruise. I felt these details, little barbs in my chest and fingers, my limbs, my gut, hooking me in. I can only talk about Novo's face in pieces. I can't put it all down in one place, the mind-numbing, accidental perfection of it. Up to my neck in him, even at that distance, happy to drown. I breathed, like I'm breathing now. Things quickened—the blood in my veins, the day's noise, more urgent suddenly, more . . . well, more everything. Novo wiped the dust off his hands, straightened up.

I knew it already. Nothing compared to this. To us.

"Jude," he said, and I said, "Novo," and that was it. Enough. He looked at me and smiled. Gap-in-the-clouds, shaft-of-sunlight wonderful. I could feel it. But I still had so many questions.

"Who *are* you?" I said. "Where did you come from? And why did you come here? To me?"

He shrugged. "I got out of a car."

"Nine thirty-four," I said.

"Yes." He smiled. "Nine thirty-four. Doesn't matter where I was before. I'm here now. We're here now. That's the point."

He scanned the houses and the yards and the hills and sea beyond. The shine on his hair was lacquer, the water at night. A pulse ticked, soft, behind his ear. He bit his lip and I thought I could taste it, and I felt all the spaces between my ribs suddenly, all my body's absences, all the ways I wasn't only me, and

I thought, *This is what desire feels like. This is why people lose their minds over it.* I had to force myself to look away. I was greedy for the sight of him, but like someone who's been starved, and has to eat slowly, take small bites, because the thing they want more than anything on earth might be too much, suddenly, for them to take.

Below us, someone smacked flies against a window and the woman opposite-but-one weaved her way up her yard with a long drink to where a deck chair sat cowering under a tree.

"Poor Henry," I said. "He's so lonely without her."

"Do you think it speeds up?" he said. "Getting old? Like, the longer you live, the smaller a part of your life a year is? Does time just get quicker and quicker and then stop when you stop or whatever?"

"Maybe," I said. "I guess we'll find out in the end."

"Maybe not."

I said, "How old is Henry, do you think?"

Novo didn't answer me.

The old gardeners were doing something with a climbing rose, shout-whispering at each other, bicker-bicker, like irritated snakes. Together we watched them. "Were those two in love once, do you think? Are they still?" he asked.

"I have no idea, Novo. So far, they just seem to fight a lot. I'm not sure they even like each other."

The look on his face was something sweet and tinged with envy, and he said, "Their garden is beautiful though, isn't it? I wonder if a whole life together feels as good as that."

I smiled at him.

"What?" he said.

"Nothing. I don't know. I'm just . . . People usually just talk about smaller things than that."

"Than what?"

"Than *that*."

"Oh. You want to talk about smaller things?"

"No. I didn't say that. I just said that people usually do. People talk about politics and football and what they did over the weekend."

He laughed. "Oh yeah? What else do people do?"

"We drink coffee and catch trains and clean mud off our shoes and reheat takeout. We watch television and take selfies and go on vacation and try to recycle."

"You don't mean that," he said. "That's not all that people do. That's bullshit."

"How do you know?" I said. "You're not people."

"No," he said. "You're right. I'm not people at all. But I want to be for a little while. Come and sit with me. Let's just sit here like people and talk small."

Up on that roof, with water ticking in the gutters and the sky the color of pearls, we talked about movies. About favorite foods and songs and colors. We wondered what dogs and cats and seagulls would say if they could speak a language we understood. We tried, really, we did. But it felt so simple. Too simple. So we gave up and instead we talked about books and the ukulele. About Bill Hicks, Gujarati cooking, the end of electricity, the I Ching, the chances of alchemy, the possibility of alien life, Tony Hoagland poems, the smell of cut grass, plastics in the Galápagos, Kintsugi pottery, the northern lights, the sea. After a while we were quiet and I watched a bee find its way into the wall through a gap in the mortar by his head. It hovered and docked like something off a space station. Novo listened. I could see him listening. He closed his eyes. "There were bees inside the wall in my last house," he said. "I used to lie in bed and listen to them. They sounded angry."

"Where was that?"

"You wouldn't know it. It was a long time ago."

"I don't understand any of this," I said.

"Stop trying to. There's more to life than what we know we know."

"I mean, there'd better be. I do hope so."

I'd left a book up there a few days ago, and the pages were now swollen and damp and all stuck together. I shook it out, laid it flat in the sun. "What are you reading?" he said.

"Just something I picked up," I said. "About hypotheticals and theories. It's like a guessing game got turned into a science."

"Like what?"

"Like time travel and parallel universes," I told him. "And black holes and quarks and the god particle. I mean. All these wild ideas, before they get broken down into equations and probabilities and stuff."

"The mechanics of magic," he said.

"Exactly. Precisely. So this is before the mechanics, when you're totally feeling your way around in the dark. Like trying to work out what the bigger picture is by studying one tiny drop of paint. Am I making any sense to you?"

"I get it."

"Gives me loads to think about."

"Tell me something you think about."

"Nothing exists in isolation, by itself," I said. "Things only exist when they are colliding with something else. Like atomically. At the very smallest level. Of everything."

Novo looked at his hands while I was talking. He pressed his palms together, interlocked his fingers.

"You see, I read that," I said. "And then I think that if it's true about atoms, and we are all made of atoms, then it must be true about people too."

"So," Novo said. "If you spend your whole life on your own you never really existed?"

"Maybe. I mean, I just think about it. Like, am I only really there when I'm talking to someone, navigating around someone, or moving through a crowd? And am I only visible from the outside, only from someone else's viewpoint a concrete, solid thing? And would I be nobody forever if I wasn't colliding with things? I like thinking about stuff like that."

"So do I," he said. "What else?"

"Well, if these atoms didn't move around and collide and stuff, which they do, constantly without a break, then everything would stop. Everything would stay the same."

"Because?"

"Because the moving about is what makes change. So without it there'd be no such thing as change. And without change there's no such thing as time, because there's no difference between the past, the present, and the future if they're all the same. And that taught me something. I mean, I'm learning something. Because I thought I hated change. You know, like angry with my mum about moving around all the time. But now I'm starting to see what's at stake, you know? What gets lost without it."

"Why do we always want something to last forever just because it's good?" Novo said. "Why can't it being good be enough?"

"Exactly. If it was all good forever, without changing, it would just be boring, right?"

"Maybe," Novo said, and I leaned into him, not too much, just a little, and he smiled and stroked my hair.

"There are as many neurons in your brain as there are stars in your galaxy," he said. "Did you know that? The potential for enlightenment and self-deception is endless."

"Well, you would know," I said. "Look at the show you've put on since you arrived."

"All for you," he said, winking.

The wind reared up suddenly, a violent sea-soaked gust, and something dropped right at me, a slate from our roof, really close. I ducked and moved out of the way quick, without thinking, and

I felt it suddenly and only then, how close I'd been sitting to the edge.

I had moved too far out into thin air, my balance tilted, and in that half instant, time stretched out like the longest piece of elastic, so long that I could take note of my own panic, as if from elsewhere, the total certainty of the hard ground way below me. I swiped at the air like it was something I could take hold of. I called out before my throat closed up, I think I called his name, and then I was fighting to get the air into my lungs, fighting to breathe even while I was preparing to fall.

Novo moved faster than anything else in that slowed-down moment as he crossed the space between us like it was never there and reached out over the roof's edge to grab both my hands. "I've got you," he said, over and over again, "I've got you," and I wanted to cry then, panic rising like lava as he pulled me up, but he put his hands on my face and the feeling cooled down, back to rock.

Above us, instant storm clouds collected, and the straight shape of heavy rain marched across the horizon in dark columns the color of slate. More and more birds filled the sky and then they were gone and the land around us began to disappear, everything lost in the slap of wind and the dark heave and shift of rushing water, like the street and the houses and the whole sky were becoming the sea. It rose up and filled the air with itself, and I could feel the wetness of it deep down in my lungs, the salt on my tongue. The rain was large and soft, kind of slow to start with, then stronger and harder until it hit us in flat, whipping sheets. I kept picturing myself at the top of that fall, tipping backward, the sudden bloom of fear as I tried to grab hold of nothing but air. Novo opened his mouth and turned his face up. Water clung in bright glass beads to the ends of his hair. He bared his teeth and spoke into the side of my cheek, and the sound of all that water swallowed up his voice, so I didn't hear him, only felt his mouth, so close, his heat on my skin.

And then, just as instantly, the clouds passed and the rain cleared and the sun was out. He looked down at himself, at his feet on the roof. I leaned into him, put my head in the middle of his chest. He was burning up.

He wiped his eyes, pushed his wet hair off his face.

"Novo," I said. "Tell me something."

"About what?"

"About you."

He thought for a minute.

"Like, really. Where are you from?"

I could see it, him weighing things up, choosing the right

words. "I'm out past those equations," he said. "I don't live in one place. Time and space are the same to me."

"But you're real."

"Yes. Course I'm real."

"Are you only real to me?"

He put his arm around me. Warm. So heavy, the weight of him. Rock solid, strangely enough.

"I'm not your imaginary friend," he said. "You didn't make me up."

"Oh, I hope not."

"But I came here for you."

"You did?"

"I've come for you before, Jude. More than once."

"What do you mean? Have we met before?"

"You've seen me."

"I have? Like I'm seeing you now?"

He shook his head. "I move fast," he said. "Speed of light has got nothing on me. You might have seen me for the infinitely smallest possible particle of a second. Almost nothing."

"But—"

"I can't control it," he said. "But we are connected. You pull me."

"How?"

"Do you want a scientific answer?"

"Maybe."

"We resonate. Our cells speak the same language. At the same frequency."

"Are you for real?"

"You pull me," he said again. "It's called love, Jude. I will always find you."

I put my hand to his face, stroked his cheek, touched his jaw. "I never believed in all that."

"In what? Love? What if it's not a question of belief?" he said. "Just equations. Like your physics."

"Is it?"

"I wait and wait for you, between times," he said, while the day carried on as normal, minute by minute, and people everywhere told stories and paid their bills and rode their bikes and tried on sneakers and thought about what to have for lunch. It didn't make any sense. I tucked my head into the crook of his arm, put my hand on his chest, the tips of my fingers on the pulse at his throat. Novo traced a line down the middle of my forehead, down my nose and over my lips and past my chin. "I'm always with you," he said. "Even when I'm not."

"I don't know what that means," I said.

"A satellite to a planet," he said. "A moon. If you can't see it, doesn't mean it's not there."

"Why me though?" I said.

"Why would you even ask that?"

"Because I want to know. What's so special about me? I mean, aren't there other bodies somewhere else, resonating in other times, with the same frequency?"

"No," he said. "There's only you."

"How come?"

"I am a lost cause," he said. "The original."

"Meaning?"

"You're my patron saint." His smile breaking, the unsticking of his mouth, the clean shine of his teeth. He closed his eyes like a cat at the top of that smile. How does the rest of the world even function without seeing that?

"You're different," he said. "Be different." And then he moved closer and kissed me. Soft, that kiss. So careful. So forever-destroyingly kind. I kissed him back, and the black-dark center of his eyes was fierce and open and hungry, and the quiet between us was something wonderful.

"Stay with me," I said. "Don't leave."

"Easy," he said, and he kissed me again. "Done, Jude. I'll do whatever you say."

We stayed out on the roof while it got dark. We stayed out all night. And later, I looked across the street for the hundredth time at his house. Doors shut, lights out, still and silent. Sunk-sunset glass above the front door, like a protractor, cataract film on all the windows, part salt air, part grime and neglect. Hard to believe Novo had scaled that wall like a lizard a few hours earlier. Hard to believe any of this at all. The house was empty now, and he was here with me. Mrs. Midler's brand-new ghosts must still be everywhere—lost lists behind the radiators, years of cooking fumes in the kitchen, cobwebs strung like bunting down the hall. I wondered how they'd like sharing their space with this new sudden spell of a boy. I wondered if they were jealous now, of me. He sat up next to me. What did we both see? The farm-dog wind, herding litter into chosen corners. The hung moon, and clouds moving blankly under the stars. Streetlights reflected in old puddles, and the huddled outline of sleeping gulls. Someone's TV flashing like lightning behind a closed curtain, a living-room storm. And each other, leaning, breathing, waiting. I had no idea for what.

In the end, he put his arms around me, shook his head a little,

and smiled, pulling me back down to sleep. The streetlight clos-
est to him buzzed half-heartedly, flickered, catching then losing
him, over and over. There, and then gone, a way of life that boy
was long used to. The far edges of the sea were on the horizon
where they belonged. The moon was high and bright, and I saw it
so clearly then. I pictured it, or I thought I did, the join between
what was real and what wasn't, for him. The fault line that he
lived on, a fluid, changeable place, like the line between the dry
land and the sea.

It didn't occur to me then that I might one day have to draw
that line for myself.

SEVENTEEN

Early morning was damp and smelled of the sea. The palm trees shivered in the breeze, tropical creatures, misfits waiting for the sun to come up. Novo wanted to go diving. We had to get our timing right because of the tides. Sometimes the caves were there and sometimes they weren't. He said they filled and emptied with the sea.

Everything seemed deserted. Like the whole world was asleep except us. I wondered if Mum and Henry even noticed I was gone.

I said, "Are we actually the only ones up?" and he said, "Maybe."

"It feels weird, doesn't it? This early in the day I always pretend the world's ended, or something dramatic, like everybody's been wiped out by a plague in the night and it's all up to me now, like I'm in my very own sci-fi film. I don't even like sci-fi films. But I can't help it."

He smiled. "And now it's happening. Just you and me."

"What are the rules?" I said.

"Rules?"

"I mean, what is really happening, and what isn't?"

"Rules are for fools," he said, and I told him, "That's a cop-out."

"I know you have questions," he said. "I know you're full of them. And questions are better than answers."

"What does that mean?"

"Questions are infinite. Like us. An open door. All potential."

"And answers?"

"They're a full stop, aren't they? A red light. An ending."

He looked at me. "We are here. We are real. Does it feel real to you?"

"Of course."

"So why are you asking? You want it locked down? You want the open door shut?"

"No," I said. "I'm just trying to navigate."

"And so am I."

No point in asking if that was a spell or not. Love is pure

magic, whoever's tricked you into it, right? I doubt it helps, finding out who's in charge.

Novo hugged me for so long, I was the one who leaned back out of it first. I was the one who felt self-conscious suddenly. I pulled away and instantly regretted it, and then I kissed him, under his chin, to feel better, and he took my hand.

We walked out of town on the coast path. Novo walked fast— long legs, big strides—and I had to work to keep up. When the path got narrow I slotted in behind and watched him move and smiled to myself that we were both there, that this was happening and he was even in that Now, right then, with me. Up at the top, the wind bit and old people sat in the still dim of their cars, looking out at the view. We ducked round the side of an ice-cream van in the little parking lot, climbed over a fence, and then half slid, half scrambled down, cutting our own path through the tough, determined shrubs that clung to the flat face of the rocks. On a wide gray ledge, flecked with bird shit, we stopped and stripped, zipping each other into our wetsuits.

The sea to our left was vast and quick and rhythmic, and below us it rolled and slapped with the same rhythm, filling and receding in this narrow deep well, this perfect blue-green O, backlit by pale sand, like the seabed itself was a source of light.

I'm not a particularly good swimmer. I'm never going to win prizes for my diving, and that O was small and impressively far below. But I was calm. I felt good. Everything was going to be fine. Better than fine. Novo leaned into the void, then dropped like a hammer into the water—immaculate, almost splashless. I took a breath. I didn't think about it. Same as the first time I saw him, he went and I just followed.

The sea when I hit it was the earsplitting cold of feedback and sheet ice and sharp metal, shocking my skin and peeling open my eyes as I drilled down. My heart stopped, my chest locked, and my brain seized, and I thought, *I am a body that's forgotten how to breathe*. Ahead of me, arms by his sides, Novo swam, sleek as a tern diving for fish. Dancing fingers of sunlight lit up his suit where they cut through the water, and he swam farther down still, and out of their reach. I couldn't feel the cold anymore. The water was no different than the air, and I didn't think about breathing or not breathing, I was just there, following Novo effortlessly down into the dark. He turned and pointed for me to look up, and above us, the refracted shapes of cloud and bird flock and cliff face loomed and swayed on the other side of the water. And all around us, the fish flashed their silver bellies when they sensed us, and flickered out of sight.

I almost lost sight of him too, in the glowering dark, and then there was new light ahead of us, getting closer, this wavering space of lit blue. Novo's body curved upward and his head and shoulders broke the surface and then so did mine. We were breathing air instead of water, and I thought, *Did I just breathe water? That's impossible*, and still I knew that it was also most definitely true.

Inside the cave, the sea echoed and popped and the sound of it bounced up high against the walls and ceiling, each drop-sound grown large, the flat hand of it slapping against the smooth stone like a rifle crack. Light flooded in stern lines through the gaps between rocks, geometric, like church light, or forest light, the sky above us the same perfect O as the circle of water where we'd dived. Novo climbed out onto a ledge and pulled me up after him into a patch of warmth, and I was cold suddenly, and my teeth began to chatter. The sea sucked and pulled itself in and down beneath us, then swelled and pressed up toward the ledge, but it was dry and warmer there and Novo put his heavy arms around me. My shivering stopped at once and I leaned into him and we were still.

"Thank you," I said, and he kissed the top of my head, breathed into my hair, rested his cheek there.

"What did I do before I met you?" I said, and he kissed me again and said, "Same as you'll do when I'm gone," and I said, "Never," and he said, "Jude. That's a terrible word."

We took off our wetsuits, and naked we were soft as velvet and so was the rock and I'm not telling you any more about it, because some of this must be mine to keep, surely, even while none of it is. So keep out, no trespassing, nobody's business.

Afterward, I had no idea how long, we both lay there, our bodies the warp and weft of each other, still holding, lullabied by the breathe-in, breathe-out music of the sea.

When I woke up the tight circle of sky above us was darker than the rock and we should have been cold, we really should have been freezing to death, but I didn't feel it. Our suits had dried and we put them back on and slipped wordlessly into the graphite-black water. Novo took my hand and he didn't let go while we swam through that blackness, and I had that feeling again, that I couldn't tell where the sky ended and the sea began, because all around us was just littered with stars.

EIGHTEEN

For a while, from the moment I saw him, there was nobody but Novo. I can't be sure how long the while lasted, but I guess that doesn't matter, because real time didn't apply to me and him. We were past that, way beyond it, astronauts circling the home planet, watching the sun rise sixteen times in a day. My absence might be nothing more than a glazing over in the kitchen while my mum talked. That's what Novo said. Time didn't stop moving without me, everything else carried on, but whole days for me and Novo wouldn't have lasted longer than it took for someone else to catch me staring off into space, for Mum to ask if she was boring me, or if I'd zoned out.

"What about Henry?" I said. "Henry will notice, won't he?"

"Trust me," he said. "You'll be there and you won't be. It's covered," and when I said, "Can you do that?" he laughed. "You know already. There's nothing I can't do."

"Oh yeah? Really?"

"And there's nothing you can't do when you're with me either. In fact, you have way more power than you think."

"Why, thank you."

We took a yacht and it sailed itself out, tiller slicing through the current, sails adjusting to the wind seamlessly while we jumped off to swim, dropping anchor when we climbed ashore to lie on every tiny bay we could find. You could do that trip a hundred times and see nothing, but with him it was different. Gray seals on the black rocks, dozens of them, pumped up and buoyant with fat, lolled in the middle of the estuary mouth, lifted their sleek heads and switched their feathered whiskers to look straight at us with their lacquer eyes. A pod of bottle-nosed dolphins slicked their backs in and out of the water and followed us, talking incessantly and opening up their laughing mouths. Novo knew the birds: cormorants, fulmars, gannets, guillemot, and razorbills. Skua, shearwater, petrel, kittiwake. Tern and falcon and raven. They flocked to him when he called them in their own voices, gathered on scraps and outcrops of rock, fussing and flapping for his attention like kids at a playground.

We walked back along the road, our shorts heavy with water and sticking to our legs like wet plaster, the cars going past us so fast I could feel the hard smack of pushed air against our bodies. Three, four inches to the right and we'd have felt the full impact of metal and engine and glass. So close, that devastation. And then the soft, quiet spaces between them, no engine, no throttle, just the air in the long grass and our feet on the tarmac, and him whistling.

We walked for days. Up on the cliffs, the narrow crumbling edges. Another fault line, another border—the land sliced and dropping straight into sea. Novo was comfortable there, at the margins of things, at the place where things change. We climbed until my lungs and my legs burned, but he wouldn't let me stop when I wanted to, would never let me stop because he could always see another place ahead, something different. Farther. Better. More.

We walked at night too, diffuse with the low, secondhand light of the moon, and we lay on our backs in the silvered grass to map stars. Novo gave me a meteor shower, because I'd never seen one. "Every time someone says they see a shooting star," I told him, "I'm blinking, or looking down, for that split second. It's not even funny." And before I'd even finished talking, the night was filled with dropping lights, and it stunned me into silence, the total quiet of all that movement, the utter vastness of the sky. I slept, and in the very early morning, wild ponies cut fast across the moor to meet us, to meet him, and we gave them grass and the cores of our apples, and Novo pressed his forehead against theirs and spoke words and they shivered with pleasure and their heads swung up when he let them go.

I remember how many stars there were out on the moor, how the wild ponies edged closer to us in the dark until we could hear their breathing and the rip of the grass they pulled out of the ground with their piano-key teeth and soft mouths. I remember how cold it got while I was sleeping, how wet everything was in the morning, like the sky had turned to liquid overnight, our quilt and blankets, my clothes soaked through and sticking to my skin.

When I said, "Thank you," he said, "For what?" like it was all nothing, all this magic, and I guess that's how we did it, how we acknowledged and overlooked at the same time how special this was, how unexpected and temporary, the solid and the unthinkable, the ordinary and the impossible-to-know. I don't think either of us knew then how long it would last. I accepted and denied his otherness, our otherness. The way you do when you're falling in love against all logic, wildly fascinating and hopelessly unrealistic, and you say, *This is not happening, no way, no thanks, not to me.*

How do I remember him right, this life-changing boy? I will never be able to do him justice, but I will never stop trying. Like the solitary soul I'd seen at the water's edge that first day at the beach, Novo was deep-down sad, the definition of lonely, and yet he laughed more than anyone I have met. He loved to be wrapped up, under a blanket, doing nothing but thinking, and he loved being outside too, moving and searching. He was tireless. Curious about everything. I realized later that I never actually saw him sleep. No detail was too small or too dull to deserve the gift of his full attention. He drank it all in, and all life came to him somehow, the way those seals and dolphins came to the mouth of the sea when he was near it, and the birds clamored and the ponies galloped to meet him. His thoughts showed on his face, when he forgot to stop them. He wrote the world down with his eyes, read situations quickly, and remembered everything he saw. Agile and daring, reckless with himself. And so careful with me. Because he was indestructible, in his own way, I guess, if I ever understood that right. And I am breakable.

I remember falling down the hill when we were smashed,

laughing till we were nearly sick, and my bruises in the morning, like tropical flowers, blue-green and purple, fading to yellow, and him, unmarked. Novo was horrified when he saw, but I thought they were magnificent. I said they didn't hurt, even though they did. I said they were worth it. And I was right.

I remember how tightly he held on to my hand sometimes, when I was touching him and he didn't want me to stop. I remember the wide fit of his fingers through mine, the lock of our mouths, the bellows-strength of our breathing. It hurts to remember that now, just like the bruises. It's hard, like I've said already. A fist in the chest.

Because bubbles burst. Heads get pulled out of the sand. Love is magic. But reality is the wall you wake up driving toward, with bad brakes. You can't avoid it. It's always coming. I know that much.

I woke up next to him, sun flooding warm through the skylight above my bed. I woke up and he was smiling and so beautiful. In that moment, he was the sum total of all the things I thought I wanted. Right then, I would have gone anywhere, without a doubt, without a backward glance, with him. And he knew it.

"Jude," he said.

"Novo."

I curled in closer to his body, the body I swear I will be able to draw from memory until the day I die. Every mark and crease and curve of muscle. Every bump and scar and stretch of flesh. He breathed out. He rested his chin on the top of my head.

The knock on the door was sudden. Hard. We both flinched. Both held ourselves dead still.

"Who is it?" I said.

Henry's voice on the other side of the door was thick with panic. The sound brought the rest of the world back with a jolt. I hadn't thought about him, or my mum, not really, not much. It could have been a year since I had seen either of them. Or a minute.

"Something's happened," he was saying. "I can't stop it. Quick."

I got up and opened the door. Henry was ragged and disheveled. Out of breath.

"What is it?" Novo said, still lying in my bed. I looked back at him and even then, even in that moment, I thought: *Just stay there. Don't move. Ever.*

"Something snapped," Henry said. "It's not working. Jude needs to come home. Now."

NINETEEN

"I am home," I said. "Look," and I sat back on my bed next to Novo, grabbed a handful of my sheets, felt the breeze from the window above us on my face, heard the gulls. My room, clean and spacious and sunlit at the top of the house. "I'm so here," I said.

"No," Henry told me. "You think you're here but you're not. You're with him. In between things. Outside them. You know this, don't you? He told you this is how it works?"

"Obviously he has," I said, but of course, I knew I didn't fully understand it.

I reached for Novo's hand. "And what if I want to be outside things?" I said. "What if I'm not ready to leave?"

Novo said, *"If,"* and he stretched and smiled and held on to my hips with his hands. "Of course you're not ready," and he looked at me, the happiest I'd ever seen him. Our last moment of pure joy maybe, the peak of the climb before downhill began, and then a little light went out in his eyes. Only small, but I saw it flicker. We both witnessed it, that peak, and we moved on, because you can't go back even if you want to. Not even Novo could go back.

"Your mother needs you," Henry said.

"My *mother*? Why? What's up? What's happened?"

Henry looked at Novo, not at me. "Did you burn through it?" he said. "Did you use the time up already?"

"What time?" I said. "What does that mean?"

Henry looked hard at Novo when he said, "It's time for answers."

"We're coming," Novo said. "Go back downstairs. Two minutes. I promise. We'll be there."

When Henry shut the door behind him, I said, "What's going on?" and Novo kissed me, hungry and fierce. He hid his face in my neck and he stroked my side, almost lazily, with the tips of his fingers, stroked my stomach and thighs. I felt him breathe in and steady himself, about to speak.

"On the beach," he said. "When you met me, I gave you a choice. Remember?"

"I do. You did."

"And you said yes."

"And I would again."

His mouth moved against my skin, warm and soft, so I felt the words he spoke as well as heard them.

"I know," he said. "I know."

We stayed there, quietly breathing, and then he got up and moved away, as decisively, as definitively as the cliff drop, and I reached after him and said, "No, not yet. Come back," but he shook his head and wouldn't look at me then.

"I can't," he said. "I really can't," and he turned away. I watched the muscles of his shoulders flex and open as he pulled on a shirt. "We've got to go."

"Tell me what Henry's talking about. What's going to happen when we get down there?"

Novo sighed. "Some things don't live very long. A mayfly has one day. A bubble breaks in seconds. The Now I kept you in lasted as long as it lasted."

"The Now?" I said. "And what? Downstairs time has carried on without me?"

He nodded, and he didn't stop watching me.

"It wasn't supposed to," he said. "I didn't think it would.

That's what Henry meant when he said something snapped. This changes things."

"Changes them how? I'm so confused."

He walked across the room toward me and we stood close, our fingers touching. I heard Henry's voice again, two floors below. I heard Mum. There was something in their voices, something coiled and tense, and I pictured it, that drama, waiting for us on the other side of the door like a primed cat, about to pounce.

"This doesn't feel right," I said.

"It's okay," Novo said. "We will fix it. And I'll be here."

"You promise?"

"On my life," Novo said. "On my life, I swear to you. I'm not going anywhere."

TWENTY

We came down the steps from the attic quietly, barefoot and half-dressed. Our tread on the stairs was light as anything, almost soundless. We were hardly there. Henry's windows were wide open, curtains flailing in the wind, and Charlie Parker was all panic-panic, hell-for-leather, in a high, far corner of the room. I heard voices again downstairs, fraught and urgent, and in my head something started ticking, a chattering feeling, like crickets, a percussive, nervous pulse. I stopped at the top of the next flight.

"I'm not liking this," I said. "I don't want to go down there at all."

Novo took my hand and pulled at me gently. "It's all right," he said. "We have to. Come on."

We got closer and I heard a chair scrape and then Mum said

something in a strangled, underwater voice that wasn't hers, and I said, "Is she crying? Is that even her?"

My mum doesn't cry. She sulks and quits eating and chain-smokes in the garden and breaks cups. But she's not a crier. This had to be something bad. Something big. And knowing that threw me. It really did.

We stopped outside the kitchen. "*What friend?*" Mum was saying to Henry in her saltwater voice. "Jude hasn't got any friends, Henry. We just got here."

I put my eye to the crack in the door. Mum was wiping her face with both hands, bleary-eyed and frantic with distress.

"It's my fault, isn't it?" she said, and even though Henry made all the right noises of dissent, she put her hands on her heart. "Something terrible has happened to my child. I can feel it in here. Jude's gone. I just know it."

"Mum," I said. "I'm right here!" and I pushed on the door, ready to reassure her. But the door didn't move, and Mum didn't hear me.

I looked at Novo. "What's going on? What's happened to me?"

"I don't know. Nothing, Jude. Look. You're here."

"But Mum thinks I'm not *there*," I told him. "What happened? Why can't she hear me?"

Henry put a fried egg on toast in front of Mum, and passed her a cup of tea. For a second, she looked down at it like she had no idea what it was. She scratched at a mark on the tabletop. The egg sweated. She pulled at the film of the yolk with her fork. It stretched out like wet elastic, and I felt the bile rise in my throat, felt it closing up small. My mum hates eggs.

"I called the police," she said. "Jude doesn't do this. It's out of character. I told them already. It's all wrong."

Novo's hand was on my back and I reached round and held on to it. There was silence in the room for a minute, and Henry turned away from the sink and everything about him was over-careful, studied—the slow rotation of his body, his feet in their slippers, parallel, pointing forward, aligned with the checkerboard tiles on the floor. His ankles were creased and swollen, like tulip bulbs. He dried his hands on a tea towel, folded it into precise quarters. His eyes locked on to mine as he looked at Novo and me through that crack in the door, through a crack in time.

"How long have I been gone?" I said, and Novo shrugged while Mum pushed her food away, uneaten, put her finger through the hot skin of her tea.

"It's just a Now," he said. "You're missing now."

"I can't take much more of this," she said, and Henry put his hand on her shoulder.

"I know. I understand."

"The only one who matters," she said. "The only one. Smart and sensitive and creative and thoughtful. Curious. Funny. Kind. Generous. I raised that kid. I love that kid. God, Henry, I love that kid."

She was crying again and I needed to make it stop. Reality is messy and it hurts people. Actions have consequences. Things happen and can't be undone. I wanted to go to her and at the same time I wanted to be back in that cave where the rocks felt like velvet and I could breathe underwater and there was no such thing as time. With Novo in a perfect bubble, without cause and effect, under the radar together where nothing but Now mattered, nothing but that. But that was over. He showed me a world of endless possibilities, just like he promised, but now I was suddenly hard up against the things we had to do.

Henry was still looking at me when he said, "Jude's going to walk through that door any minute. That's what I think."

I looked at Novo and he kissed me, passed his thumb across the flat of my top lip, and stepped away.

"Go on," he said.

"What about you? Where are you going?"

"Nowhere. Not yet."

"Not yet?"

There was a knock on the door then, and Mum jumped half out of her skin and Henry said, "I'll get it," and when he walked past us in the doorway, he said, "Come back. Now."

He opened the door to two police officers, fingers bothering their uniforms and worrying their hats while they waited for him to invite them in. They must have a script, I figured, for times like this. They must be nervous, hearts pounding, like actors stepping onto a stage. The flowers were still bright in our yard, the lawn still green, all the warm color of the morning, and when Mum stood up to meet them, there was no color in her face at all.

"Novo," I said, and I gripped his hand. "Can I be back here and still be with you?"

He smiled. "I hope so. I hope you can have everything you want. And I already told you. I'll be here," and he pushed me gently into the room where Henry was waiting, and Mum with her back turned was talking quietly to the nervous police.

She said, "I've been calling and calling. Like twenty times. And I've left messages. Nothing."

She dropped her forehead so it rested on the table and she spoke out loud to me, even though she couldn't know that I was right there, behind her, listening. "This is why you should check your phone, Jude. Why don't you just answer your bloody phone?"

TWENTY-ONE

Through the door and the light changed, and my senses felt sharper, heavier, more defined. I looked at my bare feet on the kitchen floor. I felt myself in my body like a lead weight, like a rock, and I thought, *Really, where was I if I wasn't in here?*

"It's broken, Mum," I said. "My phone's broken," and the kitchen spun and the police looked up like startled foxes and she was out of her chair and all over me, her hands on my shoulders, forehead to forehead, her hands on my face, and Henry smiled.

"What?" she said.

"You were calling me. But my phone's messed up. I think you forgot."

She didn't let go of me. Everyone was talking and I was back, I knew I was back, and I looked for Novo in the doorway behind me but he wasn't there.

"Where have you been?" Mum said. "Where the hell have you been?"

"I'm not sure," I told her, because it was the truth.

"Are you okay?"

"I don't know," I said. "Yeah. I'm okay. I'm fine."

She was smiling and crying and laughing and the police were getting up, gathering their things, and Henry was in a very still place in the corner of the kitchen, watching me.

"I'm so sorry I wasted your time," Mum said to the police, and they said, "Not at all," and everyone was smiling, and nobody seemed to know how long I'd been gone.

I asked Mum, and she looked blank, and the police were at the door already, saying goodbye, and when I asked her again, she said, "I had a feeling. A terrible gut feeling. There was this *space*, this black hole in my center, where you always are. And it was empty."

She started crying again then. She said, "It's the most terrible feeling in the world."

I thought about what Novo had told me on the other side of that door, that I was missing in the Now, and I thought maybe it was like that night horizon, this moment, no beginning or end, and that's why she couldn't tell me when it started. That's why she could only say how it felt.

"I didn't go anywhere," I said. "I think I just went to the beach and fell asleep."

She was shaking. She was too exhausted to be angry with me. Too relieved that I was back. "I panicked," she said. "I lost it."

"I'm sorry, Mum. I'm so sorry."

"You're here. That's all that matters, Jude. You're here."

She flew around the kitchen like Charlie Parker then, hardly landing, moving from place to place, all nervous energy, asking me if I was hungry, asking me what I wanted to do.

"Are you tired?" she said. "Are you all right? Do you want a shower? A bath, maybe? Shall I make you breakfast? Do you want to go out for lunch?"

The hollows under her eyes were deep gray in the spotlights. Henry and I exchanged glances.

"I think we should both sleep," I said. "When did you last sleep?"

She stopped moving. Frowned. "I can't think," she said, and then she stretched and yawned. "You might be right. I think I'm shattered."

"Me too."

She stood, slightly swaying, and reached out her hand once more to stroke my cheek.

"Go to bed," I said, and she smiled.

"Will you be here when I wake up?"

"Course I will."

She left the room and Henry pulled out a chair for me to sit down.

"Where is he?" I said. "Where's Novo, Henry? Do you know?"

"He's still here," he said. "Don't worry. You know that boy would do anything for you."

"Is he okay?"

"I'm sure he's fine."

"My body is so heavy," I said. "Like I can't carry it. I feel so strange."

"That's only natural."

"I don't understand what happened. Tell me what to do," I said, and he shook his head.

"Help me, Henry. Please. We're the same, aren't we? You and me? Can you tell me what I need to know?"

Henry sat down opposite me. "We're not the same," he said.

"But this happened to you, too, didn't it? With Dulcie."

"I'm not like you, Jude."

"What do you mean?"

"Dulcie was like you. But I'm not."

"But she was pure magic. You said so."

"She was, to me. And you are to Novo. It's you that's the miracle, Jude, to him."

"I don't understand," I said. "I thought—"

Henry spoke over me. "Novo and I are one and the same. Or we were, at one time."

"What?"

"I was like Novo once. As wild and dazzling and powerful." He smiled sadly and looked down at his hands. "But that's over now."

"How old are you, Henry?"

"Too old to be human," he said. "Not mortal like you and Dulcie. Infinite, like Novo still is, for the time being. Eternal."

"Infinite?"

He looked around the room, those eyes of his, so tired. So ancient. "The loneliness you saw in him?" he said. "On the beach?"

I pictured it then. That solitary boy at the water's edge, on the stilled beach, sighing. "Yes."

"I need you to know. That loneliness is nothing compared to

mine, with her gone, and me stuck here without her, forever."

"Forever."

"I've seen five generations come and go on this street," he said. "I've seen the town built on fields since she went. All from this window. All from this cage."

"What are you saying?"

"I am a stopped atom, Jude. The rock in the stream. Novo wouldn't tell you this, he can't. So I have to. I stayed with Dulcie because she asked me to. She chose me. I stayed because I always loved her. I love her now. I always will."

"And you were together."

"Yes. In the real world. But a lifetime in the real world is a blink of the eye for me and Novo. And Dulcie couldn't stay. Not forever."

"She left you here?"

"She died, Jude. She could do that. And so can you."

"And you've been alone ever since."

"Not just alone. Stuck. Trapped. I can't get out. Dulcie chose to be with me, she gave me one moment in time to belong to, but it meant I would be stuck here. In this Now, in this house. Always."

"Your map of the world," I said, and he smiled sadly.

"It's one way to travel. For me, the only way."

I wanted Novo with me, right then, more than anything, and at the same time, I knew for sure that it was a selfish, insatiable thing.

"He doesn't want you to know," Henry said. "He wants to stay. His whole existence is bound up with you."

"But I can't do that to him. Trap him like that. How could I?"

"I don't know, Jude. Dulcie wouldn't have done it either, if she'd known. It's why I didn't tell her. And we both paid for that. It broke her heart to leave me."

"I love him," I said.

Henry smiled at me. He took my hands in his, and those seen-everything eyes burned into mine. "And how will you do that, Jude? How will you prove it?"

In that moment, I realized the truth. But I could barely get the words out. "I have to let him go," I said. "I have to," and I felt it then, the sheer scale of that. The lifelong pain and weight as soon as I heard myself speak.

Henry just looked at me. Deeply sad, and deeply alone.

"Is there another way?" I said. "Can I go with him?" but even as I said it, I knew it wasn't that simple.

"If only it worked like that," Henry said. "But it doesn't."

"Why not?"

"Because you are the planet and Novo is your moon. If you left, it would change everything. Reality would feel it. Like a scar. You've seen. He can only come to you. He is here only for you. And you've got a whole life here."

I remembered the sight of my mother then, colorless with grief when she thought I'd gone missing. And I knew Henry was right.

It was below me, ahead of me, all around me, the Grand Canyon of loss. But still, I knew what I needed to do. For Novo. And it was the last thing on earth I wanted.

TWENTY-TWO

The last time I saw Novo, he knocked on the window above my bed. I opened my eyes and it came to me like a wrecking ball how much I loved him, how I had never wanted to feel that way about someone in my life, and now that I had, how I never wanted to stop feeling it either.

"Let me in, sleepyhead," he said, and I opened the window and he lowered himself down and pulled his shirt off, up over his soft swell of stomach, the deep cage of his ribs. The solid truth of Novo always shocked me. Larger than life. Physical magic. He lay down behind me, stretched himself out against the length of my back, his arm threading the space between my side and my elbow, his breath on the back of my neck.

I didn't know what time of day it was. I didn't even know I'd been asleep.

"Where have you been?" I asked him.

"Walking," he said.

I turned toward him, touched the planes of his face with my fingers. He still didn't know yet, what Henry had told me, what I had decided. I didn't ask any questions. And I didn't tell him.

"I missed you," I said.

He gave me a sad smile. I saw it on his face, what he was ready to give up, for me. I wondered if he saw that same sadness reflected in mine.

"I need you to do something," he said, and I said, "Of course."

He moved away from me, and only I knew that was the last time. He moved away, unburdened by that, and he got up. "Let's go."

"Where to?" I said. "What for?"

"It's time," Novo said. Nothing more, nothing less. Just "It's time."

We slipped out of the house for the last time together and we walked the center line of the road with the end of the light following, the sun's last rays spreading out in the sky behind. All the flowers in all the gardens lifted their faces in one brief show of bloom and then closed them for the night, nodding softly, tucking themselves under, saying goodbye, and the birds dipped in and out of puddles and a fox by the trash cans stopped in its tracks, the same way Novo had the first day I saw him, with nothing between us but the width of the street.

We walked away from town and up onto the cliff path and it was black-dark and moonless when Novo stopped. He let go of my hand and I couldn't see him in all that darkness, but his voice when he spoke was very close.

"Do you want to fall with me?" he said.

"Of course I do. Always. But—"

"If we fell from up here, I would catch you."

"And what would happen?"

"We'd be together. You would always have me here."

"At what cost?" I said. "What's the catch?"

"Does it matter?"

"Yes, it matters."

"Let's do it," he said. "Why don't we just do it?"

I knew that if we did, I would feel what it was like to be him. I would fall without fear and always remember falling and never, ever have to land. Not without him. Not alone. I wanted that. It goes without saying. I wanted that more than anything else. I wanted to say yes. But love isn't about what you want. Not really. Beyond that, it's about what you give. Freely. Without asking for anything back.

"Do it with me," Novo said, and I could hear the gray break of the water, way beneath us, against the rocks.

"Fall," Novo said. "Fall in love. And I'll fall with you."

For a moment, in my mind, I let us go, like birds leave the land or swimmers push off gently from the side of the pool. I let us out, together, into the air, so we were heavy, and the rushing of it past me was so quick and quickly over that I felt every part of it, can feel it still, the weight of us, the flat of the water rushing upward. I could never tell a soul well enough what that was like. In my mind, I could have done it forever, falling and not landing. It is insatiable, oblivion. Addictive, action without consequence. Falling without landing is an impossible habit to kick.

But in the real world, I stepped back from the edge. Novo didn't see it coming until it was done, my choice made, our last chance over, and there was nothing else but the word in the black air as I found my voice and told him, "No."

TWENTY-THREE

Neither of us spoke as we walked back the way we had come, to the beach. So cold. The wind pulled at the top of the water, pulled at the sand. The moon was high now, the land and the water both silver, and Novo's face when he looked at me was lightless and empty. Three cargo ships on the horizon, gray Lego blocks in the haze. We sat down on the cold ground and I stared at the line of stuff left by a higher tide—shell fragments and matte cuttlefish and the weeds lying brown like dead bracken, wet and rotten and all of it the lace-edged shape of the gone water. The sand was large and gritty. I picked up a fistful and let it leak between my fingers, and it left the palm of my hand white with fine, soft dust.

There was a cold, dark well where my stomach should have

been. I swallowed and I could taste its blackness and I hated everything then. I felt it bloom in me and it was ugly, knife-sharp, and I wanted to press the whole world out like a flame. The mass of the universe never changes, and you can't have something for nothing, and loss goes hand in hand with gain, and I knew all that but it didn't make it any better. The gulls were screaming and my spine was stretched tight as elastic and the water slapped hard at the ground. Everything in that Now was cruel. Everything tasted bitter. I wanted to scream. I wanted to break things.

Novo put his mouth against my wrist. I felt him there, his lips warm, and the soft of his tongue. He spoke into me.

"Henry told you," he said, and I said, "Yes."

He shook his head, my wrist in his hand, his mouth still on my skin. He breathed out, slow.

"Don't hate him," I said.

"Why not?"

"Because you should have told me. I deserved to know. And I needed to know to make the choice."

"And why did you make it?" he asked me.

I brought his hand to my face and I kissed his palm. "You know the answer to that."

"I will see you again," he said. "I'll always see you, even if I'm not right there with you. Even when you can't see me back."

"Do you promise? Is that true?"

"I wouldn't lie now. I wouldn't do that."

"And will I ever see you?"

"I can't tell you," he said, wrapping his arms around me, so tight, so held, it seemed unthinkable that soon he would be gone. "I don't know. But I'll be everywhere."

"I'll always look for you," I said.

He gave one last sad smile.

"How does it end? Where will you go?"

"You'll see." He grabbed my hand. "Let's go," he said. "I'm tired now."

I should have known it would have to be like that, the way he left. Something as unstoppable and inevitable and irresistible as sleep. A door between one world and another. The thing that breaks off from this Now and starts a new one over. Nothing you could argue with. Sleep always comes, in the end, and takes you, whether you want it to or not. It's what you'd die without, even if it also kills you.

At the very end, in my bed, I watched as his astonishing, electric beauty began to calm and empty, his frown dissolving, eyelids softening and going still. Such a privilege to witness. So proud that he would let me see. I felt him starting to go, almost falling anyway, until at the very last moment his whole body jumped, a controlled explosion, that drop that wakes you when you fall somewhere in a dream, that static, Frankenstein jolt. I saw it and I saw the near-miss in his eyes when he opened them, his pupils bottoming out, and I thought, *He's not going. He can't leave. He's going to stay here with me.*

"Look for me in London," he said. "I can see it. Dark and all the lights are doubled in the water on the deep-puddled road. The dips and channels are full of fresh rain, the pavements and potholes and the lull of the curb. I am waiting to cross. That's the start. I can feel the weight of the people behind me, pushing forward, thinking ahead, always ahead. This little island in the road is crammed with them, full to capacity and more coming. A taxi takes the corner close, the bus after it at a wider angle, and then a white van hits a puddle just right and sends the water in a high arc like an opening fan.

"You are next to me, reading a book. I feel you there before I see you. All this noise and downpour and rush hour and thunder and you are standing at the very edge of the curb, older than you are now, separate and quiet, just reading. There are raindrops on your glasses and in the wet they are slipping and you push them back to the bridge of your nose and you aren't there, not really, not in this darkening street on this grimy, beautiful evening. Neither of us is there. You are no more there than I am. You are lost in that book.

"The island crowd surges forward and the surge pushes you into the road, tips you over the square edge, thoughtless, and the driver trying to beat the lights hasn't noticed you tipping, your center of gravity shifted already, the start of your fall. Not high, that curb, but dangerous enough. Behind me, somebody sees you. Somebody gasps, and the car chases down the space between you, heads straight for you as you look up from your page and meet reality in that heartbeat, take it all in. I can move faster than any car. My arm is a turnstile, unyielding. I stop you. It's what I am here for, to stop you. To keep you safe, in your book. It sweeps past, and I pretend that you will remember it, when I'm gone—won't be long now—I tell myself that you will remember the strong shut gate of my arm."

I wanted him to say something more, to keep talking, but he didn't. He looked at me and he opened his arms and I lay against him, and in the end, we closed our eyes at the same time and our breathing fell in together and it was calm and soft and slow.

Neither of us said a word in that Now, while the universe went on expanding beyond belief all around us, because we knew that what we said next would have to be the perfect thing, or nothing at all.

TWENTY-FOUR

I dreamed it was the first of July. I knew it before I knew it, and I was reading in a patch of sunlight, without taking in the meaning of the words. Nine thirty-three and in my dream I was expecting Novo to get here, tall in his black clothes, in his big black car. I was in that Now and I was also watching it, lining it up next to so many others, thinking, *This is how it will go.* The garbage truck in the road, jaws grinding. Someone's cat in a patch of sunlight. The gulls and the old happy-ever-after couple and the woman opposite-but-one and Henry this time, the only difference, a Henry I knew better than anyone, somewhere in the house, calling my name. I held my breath and I waited, and every leaf and feather and blade of grass waited with me, for the thing that was about to happen. Red letter, highlighter pen, page corner, clear as glass. But Novo didn't come, and something was swallowing me at the edges when I woke up, something vast, all that absence.

Alone in my bed, the memory of him was still there on my body, only hours old. His warm breath, the soft meat of his flesh, the inside of his elbows, the taste of his mouth. I heard his voice and his catching laughter. I saw him smiling, saw the glint in his quick, dark eyes.

That's all I can say about that, hitting overwhelm, falling apart. When you're swallowed by a whale you can't talk about it until it spits you out, until it lets you go, and you remember to swim up and try looking for the light.

TWENTY-FIVE

Later, Henry knocked on my door and I didn't answer but he came in anyway, and he pulled a chair up to the edge of the bed and sat down.

I kept my eyes closed and I listened to him breathing and we were quiet like that for a long time, because I had nothing. I was nothing. I didn't know what to say.

Novo's face was filling my head, getting closer and closer until he wasn't his likeness anymore, just a dark collection of shapes, and I remember thinking, *Is that what he is now—not the same, not here, but somewhere else entirely, diffuse, like ink in water? And is that what I have to hold on to, best-case scenario? All I can hope for?* I pictured myself destroying everything—this room, this house, this stupid little town—and I breathed and breathed and waited for the film of it to stop playing on a loop in my head.

"Talk to me," Henry said.

"You're the only person who knows," I said.

"Yes."

"You're the only one I can talk to."

"That's why I'm here."

"I'm so tired," I told him. "I don't think I've ever been this tired."

"I know," he said.

"He's gone, Henry. I sent him away. I have to carry that forever now."

A lost cause, lifelong burden, same as my stupid, sad name.

"I know, Jude."

I opened my eyes and stared at the ceiling and my tears ran straight down onto my pillow, pooled quietly in the cups of my ears.

"What happens next?" I said. "What am I supposed to do now?"

Henry shifted in his chair. He cleared his throat and spoke quietly. "Time will pass unbearably slowly," he said. "The days will feel worn out before they start and lead-heavy and there will be no room for the size of what you feel."

"*Nothing compares*, you said."

"No, Jude. Nothing will. And you will feel like there will always be something wrong with you—the same hurt, the same lack—and that the feeling will last forever, until you stop feeling anything at all."

I sat up. "Help me," I said. "I made the wrong decision."

"No, you didn't."

"Well, it feels like that. I don't know what to do."

"Why did you let him go?" he asked me.

"What?"

"You wanted to fall with him."

"Yes. Of course I did. I still do. I still want it."

"So what stopped you?"

"You did," I said. "You told me the truth. I couldn't trap him. I couldn't do that, not to him."

I lay on my bed and looked up at the sky and I remember thinking it had no sense of occasion, no business being so blue.

"But I can't do this either," I said.

"You will be sad," Henry said. "Of course you will. For a long time, Jude. And you must be."

"I'll never not be. And what about him?" I said. "I worry about him. How he is feeling. He'll be so lonely, Henry. He'll be the loneliest."

Henry sighed. He patted my arm. "Didn't he tell you that he's always known you?"

"Yes."

"Did he tell you he's found you before? The other times you met?"

"Yes," I said. "He told me."

"And did you know that he was there? At the time?"

"No, of course not. I didn't know him until this time."

"So how can you be sure that he's not here right now?" Henry said. "I mean, here, in this room, right now, for the smallest possible fraction of a second? How could you know that he will never be with you again?"

"Is that possible?"

Henry laughed, just a little. "You and I both know for a fact that everything is."

"You promise?" I said.

"Trust me, Jude," Henry Lake said. "The worst has already happened and you are still here. Still breathing. You did the right thing."

I was quiet then. I hated how awful doing the right thing made me feel.

"Those pins on the map," he said. "They were places Dulcie

and I could only talk about, at the end. Could only dream about seeing. The grief she felt, every day, when she saw what was going to happen to me, without her. I had her. A whole lifetime. And now I'm stuck. I can never move. Never change. Only grow older and never die. And I would do it again. I would give her everything. I had no choice. But she did. She just didn't know what it would cost me."

I listened. I wanted what he said to filter through what had set inside me, like the way water drips through rock and changes it. I wondered if it would take as long.

"The catch," I said. "The downside."

"Novo came for you," Henry said. "He would have given up his life. Same as I have. But you saved him, Jude. You saved him. You freed him. And yourself too. I have never been prouder of anything or anyone in my endless life. And one day, yes, I promise, because of that, you are going to be fine."

TWENTY-SIX

Henry Lake was right. Of course he was. I survived the equation of love plus loss. I am fine. I'm still here. Still bleeding. It starts off in a parallel place, recovery. Like when you're lying in bed and everything is bone-heavy and the sky has no business being blue and you don't see the point of any of it but you picture yourself, a part of yourself, getting up and eating breakfast and getting on with your day like you ought to, and then one day you do it. One day you actually do.

He offered me a way out before I wanted one.

"I'm a rich man," he told me, a few months after Novo, when everything still felt like a bruise and it was all I could do to get out of bed in the afternoon and put one foot in front of the other. "I'm a rich man with nowhere to go. All I have are these pins on a map. When you're ready, if you are ever ready, come to me and I'll help. We can plan your next adventure."

There was a morning.

I walked out of town alone on the coast path and when it got narrow I put one foot in front of the other and I smiled to myself that I could do this, that I had come this far without Novo and that this was happening. Life was happening again. Just to me. On my own.

Up at the top, a different wind bit and different old people sat in the still dim of their cars, looking out at the view. The ice-cream van hunkered down against the cold blasts, its generator humming and grumbling. I ducked round the side of it in the little carpark, climbed over the fence, and half slid, half scrambled down that same path to the wide gray ledge flecked with bird shit.

The sea to my left was vast and quick and rhythmic, and below me it rolled and slapped with the same rhythm, the whole world on a loop, filling and receding in that narrow deep well, that perfect blue-green O that Novo had brought me to, backlit by pale sand, like the seabed itself was a source of light.

I was scared this time, because I was alone, and he couldn't save me. But I pretended not to be. I told myself I wasn't. I told myself that the time with him in it was still happening some-where. We were still in it. I could be without him, be without the object of love and still have the love. Mine to keep. That's what I told myself.

I leaned into the void and instead of diving I jumped and the water when I hit it was still the earsplitting cold of feedback and sheet ice and sharp metal. And my heart stopped, my chest locked, and my brain seized, and I thought again, *I have forgotten how to breathe*, if I was thinking anything at all. And then like a cork I came back to the surface and the ear split was my own voice this time, laughing and squealing, shouting at all of it, telling myself, "Again! Again! Oh my GOD, Jude! AMAZING. Let's do it again!"

And that's when I knew that I could go anywhere. Be any-where. And that I had to. Because by letting him go, I had set us both free. Both of us. Not just Novo. And that freedom is the antidote to heartbreak. The only known cure.

I went straight home to tell Henry, and Mum was on her way out to work. A changed woman, my mum. A good job. A town full of friends. This last move had been the best thing for her.

"Good swim?" she said, messing up my salty hair. "The suntan on you, Jude. You look good. You're looking better."

"I'll walk with you," I said, and she put her arm around my waist, and we went down the path together and opened the gate. Across the road, Mrs. Midler's house had new owners. They didn't know a magic boy had scaled the face of it like a lizard. They had no idea I had watched him sit on the highest windowsill, and followed him into town, and that everything else had sprung from that moment, everything I felt and thought and was.

"What's your plan?" Mum said, and she meant, like, that afternoon, but I told her anyway.

"I'm going away," I said.

"Really? Where?"

"You know. Traveling. I want to see some World."

She looked at me for a second. "Good idea."

Passed the war memorial and the charity shop. Mum smiled at me. "Henry will be pleased," she said.

"What did he tell you?"

"He's been waiting," she said. "He wants to help you."

And that was it. It was that easy. When I started out, I was just walking. I had no idea what I was doing, honestly, only a need to shut the door behind me and go, because it was time, now I'd decided, to get on with the business of living. Mum and Henry waved me off at the door, still drinking the champagne that Mum had splurged on, her chanting, "Postcards, postcards, POSTCARDS!" at me, all the way up to the corner of the road, where I turned and waved, and blew kisses and stepped on my own out into the world and kept going.

I took a bus, sat at the back, watching the raindrops gather and collect in quick lines on the windows, the kid desperate beyond everything to get out of its stroller, the old man muttering to himself, and the girl in tears on her phone. At the station, I stood on the freezing platform and waited for whatever train would be coming from the left, trusting my instincts over my sense of direction. Trusting my gut. Even now, the way I feel isn't swallowing me up if I keep moving. It's the only cure I've found for what I've lost. Going somewhere. Anywhere. All the time. In my head I see stampedes of horses, torrents of water, jet planes, spacecrafts, all light speed and hurtling. I think about Superman, flying round the earth so fast that he slows it down on its axis, stops time and all that. It's ridiculous, impossible, I know, but I can't help it, because ridiculous and impossible have been given whole new definitions for me.

At the airport, I couldn't sit still. Part of me wanted to run home and never leave, like Henry. The rest of me smiled at everyone, delighted with this brand-new self, this healing of wounds and shedding of skin. After takeoff, I relaxed, almost, breathing out into the cabin, making my donation to the noisy, communal air. The way I feel about Novo was in everyone's overhead bin then, everyone's seat pocket, everyone's lungs. I thought, *We are all in it now*, the traveling toward a life, five hundred miles an hour, at thirty-five thousand feet.

It's love, I told myself. It's love, for god's sake, and who doesn't want to be a part of that?

TWENTY-SEVEN

And so I travel. The windows on this train fill the space between the bunks, big as flat-screen TVs. If I lie on my front I can look out at everything we're passing, once it's light enough. The man across from me is stretched out on his side like a prince, curvaceous and plump. He frowns and pouts and looks down at one of his three phones. In my head I list all the old-school stuff that used to fill the world with weight and object and now fits inside a phone instead. Barometer. Calculator. Camera. Notebook. Telescope. Newspaper. Calendar. Radio. Map and compass. Watch. Wallet. TV. Voice recorder. Heart-rate monitor. Bank. I'm not tired of it yet, and I'm not nearly done. "Unbelievable," Novo said once. "What a compact time to be alive."

When the boy comes through with the chai, the prince flicks

at him with the back of his hand, curls his lip, and doesn't speak, but the boy knows what it means and pours him some and takes the money in silence, eyes down. I have some too, half a tiny cup. I thank him and my voice is louder than I expected in the quiet train. Conspicuous.

I was lucky to get a bed. My ticket didn't count, apparently, didn't exist. I handed my booking in at the desk, once I'd found the right one (third time lucky, up a flight of stairs, foreign tourists only, who knew?). Behind me and below me, Mumbai Central Train Station swarmed and hollered and sprawled. The upstairs waiting area was quieter, hushed even, like a library. I waited my turn, melting already in the winter heat, pretty sure that the only people who actually wait in line for anything in Central Train Station are the foreign tourists, and that's why we get a room of our own, because otherwise we are never, ever going to get it together to leave. I used to hate waiting in line. But these days, there are plenty of Nows in a wasted hour for me.

At the counter, I handed over the paper. An eye roll, a headshake, a sigh. The ticket man scratched his belly and didn't bother looking up from his screen. He'd clearly had this conversation too many times already, with too many clueless travelers like me.

"Waiting list status," he said. "No berth, no seat," and he didn't tell me why, because he didn't have to.

I swear it wasn't unwelcome, this feeling that my plans were falling apart already. I'm half-sunk into the unknown on purpose, have been from the beginning, soft and accommodating, like a bog. The man said I should come back later, give it three hours and there'd be room. So I took his advice. Three hours to kill, no different than the ones I'd been killing at home all that time since Novo left. Mum told me once that when I got to be her age I wouldn't get over how much time I'd squandered—how much I'd give to claw some of it back. According to her, there are about six hundred thousand hours in the average lifetime, and I'd already spent way too many of mine sulking around in my sweats and beached on the sofa. True enough. I couldn't argue with that. But I had my reasons. I told her if that's what she thought, it was a mystery she ever bothered ironing pillowcases or vacuuming the crap out from behind the cooker. When she laughed, I didn't raise the possibility that there was also such a thing as an extraordinary lifetime, the opposite of average, not straight, start to finish, like an arrow, but numberless and infinite like a wheel.

To use up three of my hours, I took a cab driven by an economics student called Dev to Rampart Row and drank a fresh lime soda, sweet and salt, no ice, at a tourist bar, all winter-scene murals and plastic tables and cooled air. I sat near the door to watch the street—wiry dogs and car horns and hot traffic, whole families on mopeds, women at the back, sari skirts dancing like flags in and out of the wheels. I saw a man sitting up against a blood-red wall, legs straight out in front of him, the stumps of his feet all bandaged and seething with flies. Two little girls walked past him, oblivious, breathing secrets into each other's ears, covering their mouths with their hands when they laughed.

I felt my heart in my chest then, still there, still beating, in spite of everything, and I thought about how many times it's done that since it was made, how many more beats it will make before I'm finished, the exact number, written down on a scrap of paper for me to read. What kind of a difference would it make in the world if that was a number we all knew? And what does it change, what kind of person does it make you, if you know for sure that the number is infinite, that you and your beating heart are never ever going to stop?

But still. I've done it. I'm on the other side of the world going somewhere. I'm not stuck on the sofa at home, staring into space. I'm here on this train staring out of the window. Always moving, always learning, living a life, as instructed. The only way.

This train bumps and thrums like a heartbeat, soothing, actually, pulling me down to sleep. I think about other numbers. How many stops between Mumbai and Madgaon. How many miles an hour this thing will go while I am sleeping. How many minutes it will wait at each station and how many people will get on and off. The number of days I knew Novo for, and all the useless days before I knew him, and all the endless days since. The number of nights we spent awake and talking, just talking, as if no one had ever quite heard our voices before. The weight of all he did and didn't tell me. The sheer volume of our laughter. How many people he will see in his own lifetime, compared to mine. How long it will be, if ever, before I forget about him and about how this feels, before I'm whittled down and worn out by experience and disappointments and other loves (not like this one, nothing like this one) and can throw in the towel and say, "I knew a boy once."

I put my face up against the window, keep the light out with my hands, and try to see what we are moving through, what kind of place—a suburb, a slum, a farm, a forest, a river. It's too dark out there, black-dark, but this is not all I've come down to— looking and looking and the whole time not seeing a thing. My eyes are open. I drink this stuff in. Something tells me the world is full of magic and I will learn how to love everything in it, except for Novo, because that is the only way to love him, in the end.

My name is Jude, I tell myself, and I let him go, that magic boy, and we are both free.

The lack of him feels as real and as solid as his body beside me once did.

Hello Now, I tell him, *wherever you are*.

TWENTY-EIGHT

I used to think everything in life was a choice, but love was never a choice for me. Novo arrived, dark and unfathomable in that beginning, like looking over the pier at night and not knowing how far down the water is. And still, somehow I knew him. I knew who he was without even trying, and even though that's impossible, even though I shouldn't believe it, that right there is my truth. I could have told you straightaway that Novo wasn't born like the rest of us, but forged in some mythical foundry out of horses and squid ink and velvet and sail rope and butter and gold. And here he was, contained in that body like a genie in a bottle, looking the lesser flesh-and-blood mortal that was me straight in the eye. A shot glass, a cold blast, a breath of fresh whatever. Novo, Novo, Novo, the perfect name for the one who still wakes up time after time, brand spanking new.

In the end, I could have watched him all day. I could have spent my whole life doing it, gladly, you know? Watching him do the ordinary things that he gilded just by doing them. Novo making a cup of Lapsang tea with honey so that it was the only color, the only level of sweetness and smoke that a cup of tea should ever be, and I could never imagine drinking anything else. His fierce frown, and the way his mouth opened ever so slightly when he thought of something to say, while that something was his still, and he hadn't given it up yet. He was so definite about everything, so purposeful, so sure. God. His way of holding a glass. Or a knife. Or a pen. I am mad jealous of the things Novo touches now. I envy the air his hands move through when he's telling a story. Wherever he may be.

Here are three words that don't even begin to cover it: I miss him. But then I missed him from the moment we met, because even before it started I knew it would have to end. I was certain of that, without having to ask. Just like life, how we all know we're going to die at some point, but we go ahead and feel the thing anyway, and do our best to make something of it before it runs out, so it's not for nothing.

Until we find ourselves at another beginning. Another Now.

That first day on the beach, when it had only just begun and was still already on its way to being over. That's what started it. A roller coaster right at the start—no time for second thoughts, locked in, holding on, paid up for the ride—and quick when you look back. So quick you want to do it all again.

I remember.

"Hello Now."

And I said, "What?" because all life was so loud in my ears suddenly, I didn't think I'd heard him right.

"Oh, and look," he said, smiling, not just at me, but at all of it. "Here's another Now. Hello to that one too."

He took that stupid, half-dead, not-even-functioning phone out of my hands and said that instead of pinning it down for later, maybe I should just try being in it for once. He said there was a Forever in every Now, if I was only willing to see it. "You're missing it, Jude. You're missing it the whole time."

And that's how he nudged me out of the real world and over into that moment, that particular Now, with the tide going out and the birds breaking the surface of the water, and the unrepeatable light and the warmth of us on that cold sand, not touching, not yet, but near enough, and like I said never-ending, already done.

"Hello Now," Novo said as I moved atom by atom toward him, irreversible, and I said it back, and he said it again and we were like the flat, constant waves then. Hello Now, Hello Now, Hello Now.

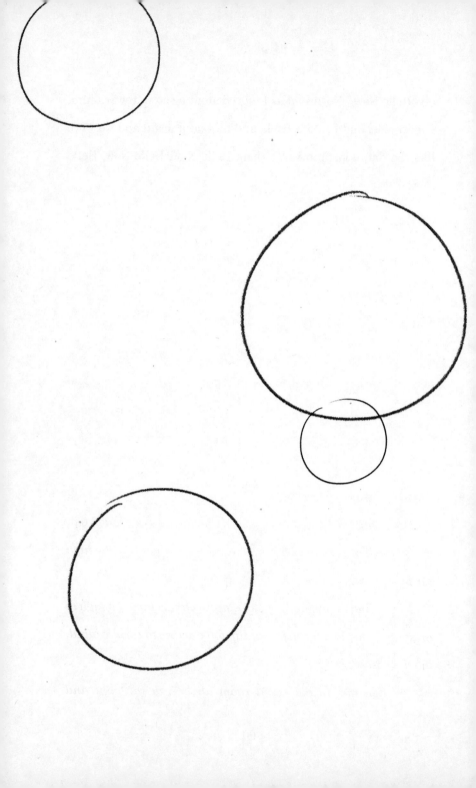

Novo

I am in a great room lined with doors. I have no idea how I got here, no memory of the door through which I entered. The room is so long that I can't see where it ends. I can't be sure that it does. Each door is identical to the next, and there are so many it will take a lifetime just to count them.

All I can think of is escape.

The first door I try stands over a canyon so deep that I can feel the pull of the fall, the hum of it in the doorframe, the high air pushing against me as I force it closed.

The second door shows me an empty cell just large enough to crawl into, too low for me to sit up, too narrow to turn around, too dark to see.

Through the third I see a room alive with the glint and

whistle of flying knives, so many and so effortlessly sharp that anyone passing through it would be cut into fine slices.

The fourth, fifth, and sixth doors open onto solid walls.

The seventh to an explosion.

At the next, a pack of starved dogs lunge at me, their teeth and claws savaging the door's skin as I slam it, a finger's width from my face.

Behind other doors flames that burn hot on my skin, a stampede of frightened horses, a floor slick and writhing with a million dying fish.

One door leads to another endless room lined with doors, and I shrink from the sight of it with exhaustion and horror.

Whole days and nights will pass as I open these doors and close them again. Time changes. Even without windows or a view of the world I know that the sun somewhere is rising and setting, and that the moon shows more and then less of its face.

I will grow weak and tired. My clothes will fall from the bones and angles of my body like I just hung them out to dry.

And as my strength fails, I know finally that there is no end to it, no escape, and that all I can do is choose or keep searching.

And the next door moves just before I can touch it, opened from the other side by a gust of air. By something I can't see.

This is my door. I know it without question.

I go through.

And when it happens, I don't feel it. I never feel it. I just sleep. And they wash away, the things I've held on to, all of them. I let them go, leave them unchanged, and they are clean and new and nothing and then I am back. Never the same place—sometimes the cut and pulse of human traffic, sometimes a vast empty space. Anywhere and Always. The hot bite of dust, a blanket of snow. Soft opening of a morning or deep, sharp night. Sometimes before Now, and during, and also after, just the land holding bodies and the birds rising up over the sea. Square one, in all its different disguises. Always moving. Always alone.

I never forget what I am looking for, over and over, somewhere in that black-hole sleep. The one that keeps me. The one I can keep. My hook. A face at a window, the air in a bubble, a bird in a cage. Consequence. Purpose. Belonging. Your feet in the grass, Jude. Your face at a window. Your hands, your mouth, your smile.

A street. Here. Now.

Will it be this time? Will it be never? I will know my name and my age, my own hands, all my histories, same as ever.

Quiet facts come to me like old finger drawings on glass, only traces. These trees. This house. This beginning. I stand at the side of the road, taking it all in, hoping and hoping. And I wonder, not for the first time, if it has some kind of start, this life, and who's controlling it, and if it is ever, ever going to stop.

I will remember everything. I will write it down in my memory and keep it. And then I will sit, unnoticed, pretending not to wait.

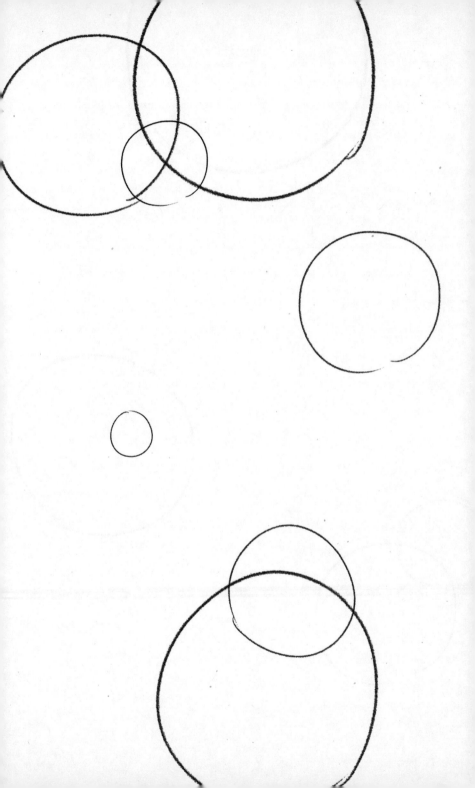

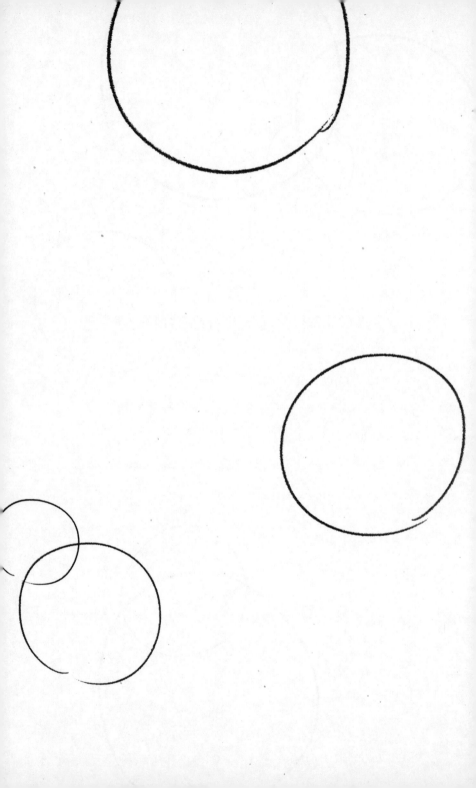

Acknowledgments

THANKYOU THANKYOU THANKYOU to

Rachel Denwood, Veronique Baxter, and Liza Kaplan

Chrissy Philp

And Gabrielle Walker, who read way too many uncooked versions, and is still talking to me anyway.

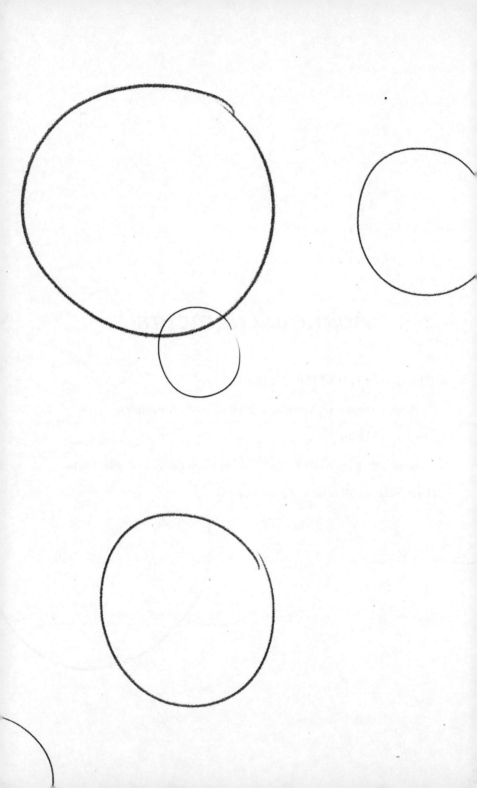

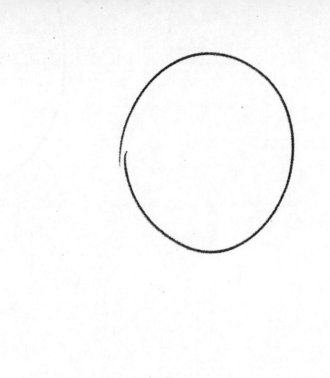

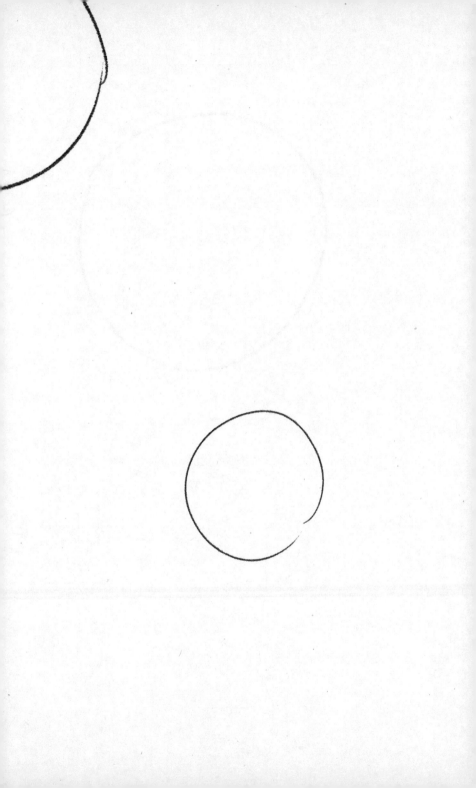

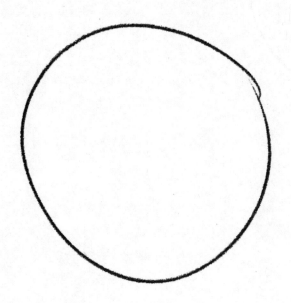

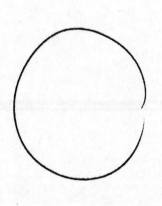